BEAR AT SEA

A Bear Jacobs Mystery

Linda B. Myers

About This Book

Bear at Sea is a work of fiction. Names, characters, places and happenings are from the author's imagination. Any resemblance to actual persons – living or dead – events or locales is entirely coincidental.

No part of this book may be used without written permission, except in the case of brief quotations in critical articles and reviews. Email inquiries to myerslindab@gmail.com

Published 2017 by Mycomm One

© 2017 by Linda B. Myers

ISBN: 978-0-9986747-0-4

Book Design by IntroStudio.me

For updates, news, blog and chatter:

www.LindaBMyers.com

Facebook.com/lindabmyers.author

www.amazon.com/author/lindabmyers

myerslindab@gmail.com

Dedication

For my sister, Donna Whichello.

Bear doesn't have a clue without her help.

PREFACE

It's quiet now. Eunice and I are both in our beds, needing sleep but it won't happen. Sorrow steals your ability to turn off your brain. I keep playing the whole thing over and over in my head. I cannot conceive of the how and the why. But I'm getting ahead of myself. I need to start before the day went so wrong.

- Lily Gilbert, Assistant to PI Bear Jacobs

INTRODUCTION

The Japanese feather industry damn near plucked the short-tailed albatross population to death. Volcanic eruption at the bird's breeding ground took its toll as well. But WWII really did the trick. Somewhat understandably, the welfare of the albatross was not a top concern at the time. After the war, an American researcher visited Japan's Torishima Island and declared it to be barren of the birds.

But he was wrong.

Juveniles had been growing up while soaring over the Bering Sea during the war years. They flew for months on end, producing a stomach oil that made an energy rich food. Along the way they desalinated their own bodies. When they matured enough to require mates, they returned to the island to breed. Japan and the United States took measures to save them. Today, a fragile population still flies the North Pacific skies.

They were called fool birds by Japanese and boobies by Americans because the albatross is awkward on the ground. They also allow humans to get close enough to kill them. This name-calling might better have been aimed at the people who labeled them. The tail of the short-tailed albatross is no shorter than its relatives, even longer than some. But if they were called long-tailed, then the entity formed to save them would have been called the Protective Association of the Long-Tailed Albatross or PALTA.

And everyone can agree that PASTA is a much catchier acronym.

CHAPTER ONE

Case Notes
May 3, 11 a.m.

Eunice Taylor has always been fond of pasta. But it's not the kind served here at Latin's Ranch Adult Family Care on Sicilian Night that I'm talking about. It's PASTA as in the Protective Association of the Short-Tailed Albatross. Turns out she's a sitting duck for an albatross, so she - and her money - have taken on the PASTA cause big time. Donations, sure. Plus a whopping big endowment for the future.
She surprised everyone but me with an announcement at breakfast one morning not long ago. She held up a photo of a white bird with a blue-tipped pink beak. "This is a short-tailed albatross. These beautiful birds are drowning, caught on hooks or tangled in long-lines dragged by fishing boats." Her false eye lashes fluttered and she patted her silk kaftan in the general area of her heart.
"I'll be damned," muttered Bear Jacobs as he buttered a warm corn muffin. "Could you pass the honey, Lily?"
He could have at least acted like he was interested.
Eunice would not be sidetracked. "It happens to a hundred thousand boobies a year all around the globe." Her orange spiked hair trembled in sympathy with her lower lip.
"Imagine that. A hundred thousand boobies," said Charlie Barker, plopping a dollop of guacamole on his huevos rancheros. "I'd give

my eye teeth to see just one nice set again before I die."
"That's not funny, Charlie Barker," Eunice snapped.
"It is not wise for you, this interruption of my little dove," Frankie Sapienza said, staring icicles at Charlie. If the two hadn't been friends, the old capo would have stared something scarier. Like daggers.
"All right, no harm meant," Charlie replied, holding up both hands. "No need to mobilize the mob."
Eunice patted Frankie's hand then resumed. "Through PASTA, I have supported the introduction of by-catch mitigation devices in the North Pacific."
"A by-catch mitigation device. Is that a marital aid?"
"Charlie," growled Bear. "I suggest you let Eunice say her piece and get it over with."
"Thank you, Bear. By-catch mitigation devices are specialized hooks and lines that can save birds or fish that were never meant to be targets. The poor things can disentangle themselves and go free. It's for my efforts on the birds' behalf that I have been awarded PASTA's Arctic Angel Award. I pick it up in a ceremony in Juneau, Alaska on May 18."
Eunice paused for effect. She straightened her back and may have puffed out her chest although the kaftan hid that particular bit of body English. She spread her arms in a graceful movement as though trying to encircle us. "And you're all coming with me!"
Silence while we all looked at Eunice then at each other. Not one of us is on the south side of seventy-five. And not one of us gets around without some help from a fall-on-your-ass mitigation device. Well, except Eunice. Maybe she's forgotten that even though she's an octogenarian, she's spryer than the rest of us.
"Just how do you think we're gonna do that?" asked Bear, who was the only trained investigator in the breakfast room. As his assistant, I keep these case notes. Not that they're real case notes. There isn't a real case, at least not yet. But leave it to a retired private investigator to probe for answers.
"By cruise ship, of course!" Eunice said in the same bright tone she would use to yell 'surprise' at a party. "And I'm paying for the whole thing."

CHAPTER ONE

> *"Juneau?" asked Frankie. He stared at 'his little dove' as though she'd just become his little dingbat.*
>
> *"Cruise?" asked Bear. His frown deepened the plenty-deep lines in his frowny face.*
>
> *"Free?" asked Charlie in delight.*
>
> *"Yes. A cruise ... to Alaska ... and it's free," answered Eunice, nodding from one to the next. "We leave week after next."*
>
> *"Did you know about this?" Bear swung toward me, his lower jaw jutted out.*
>
> *"Me? Why would you think I wouldn't tell you about a thing like this?"*
>
> *Of course, I'd been carrying Eunice's secret while she planned it all out and prepared to deal with the million objections that would follow. I must say I consider Eunice, like the short-tailed albatross, a pretty rare bird. It's hardly her fault that her long association with the bird was soon to lead to 'murder most fowl' for the Latin's Ranch gang.*
>
> *- Lily Gilbert, Seafaring Assistant to PI Bear Jacobs*

Retired PI Bear Jacobs sat at the game table waiting for the others to assemble in the living room for their trip to the senior center. The Latin's Ranch regulars went twice a week to socialize and to give Jessica Winslow, the owner of the adult care home, a little time off from senior sitting. While he waited, Bear was feeding Baby Benny. Baby Benny was seeing just how far he could spit his oatmeal.

"I knew people at the nursing home who acted just like you, champ," Bear muttered. "We're not done 'til you get more of this goop inside than out."

Benny made a facial gesture that Bear chose to interpret as a smile. Jessica had said the baby was sleeping better now and seemed happier more of the time. Bear could feel his iceberg of a heart melt just a bit at the baby's drooly smirk.

"Stay out of the casinos, kid," Bear said. "You got no poker face at all."

Bear was one of Benny's favorites. The old man could have been mistaken for a stuffed version of his namesake. His head was round, his eyes dark as black beads, his brown beard and hair shot through with gray. His arms were a genuine bear hug that held the baby safe from a dangerous world. They often sat together when Jessica needed a helping hand.

Nobody spoke of it, as though talk could make it real. No need to court disaster. But Bear knew all the residents hoped for the same thing: that this baby would rise above the crack and booze that may have poisoned his system in the womb. Their caregiver Jessica was Benny's mother now. She and Ben Stassen had adopted him after Ben's daughter disappeared back onto the Seattle streets, leaving her baby behind.

Bear was making yummy noises that Baby Benny was ignoring when the big man heard the sound of Lily's cane tapping the floor. "Just look at these beauties," she said as she walked into the room holding a vase bursting with reds, yellows and whites. The strong aroma of species roses wafted into the living room with her. Bear knew she loved to be out on the patio, working with their container garden. He figured a fresh breeze was responsible for the pink in her cheeks and her disorganized cloud of white hair.

Charlie looked up from the sports page and smiled. "Still a pleasure to see you walk into a room, Lily. It's a sight to behold."

"One of these days, Charlie, I may even skip like a little girl." Lily had received her new prosthetic leg at the start of the year. She'd pushed through pain and fear of falling and threats of deadly infection that could manifest where the artificial and the real leg joined. At facing down problems with dogged determination, Lily was a rock star. Her wheelchair was a thing of the past, and she only used her rolling walker at times when she removed the prosthesis. Otherwise, she employed a cane to help her with balance. Her physical therapist said she'd always feel more secure with one. Then he'd shrugged and added, "Of course, I'm thinking of normal people."

Eunice came into the room just after Lily, a sprig of clematis tucked over an ear. Rhinestones in her sunglass frames twinkled and little bells in her earrings tinkled. "It's gorgeous outside. And so warm I only need a shawl." She was wrapped in an eye-popping red and black scarf with the Salish tribal art pattern of hummingbirds. "Every blooming thing is having a field day. Even the horses are racing around the pasture feeling their oats."

"Eunice," Bear said, interrupting her song of spring in a far less lyrical voice.

CHAPTER ONE

She stopped. In fact, his tone was serious enough that they all looked up. "Yes, Bear?"

"About this cruise."

She bloomed again. "Doesn't it sound fun? I have brochures we can share at the senior center today." She patted the tote bag she carried, the one she'd Bedazzled with GOOD VIBES.

"Guess I don't need to wait 'til then to tell you." He wanted to get this over with.

"Tell me what, Bear?" Eunice took a seat next to him at the game table, looking like a worried ginger poodle. Baby Benny made a grab for her tote, a fat little fist wrapping around the blingy strap.

"I'm not going."

"What?" said Charlie, Lily and Eunice, pretty much in unison.

"It's very generous of you, Eunice, but it's not for me. Cruising."

"Why not?"

"Spent time in troop carriers in Nam, you know. Never much liked boats ever since."

"Oh! But this isn't a boat ride, Bear. This is a luxury *ship*. Taking people to beautiful places."

"Never much liked people, either, come to think of it."

"All your friends will be there," Eunice said, once again holding her arms wide to include everyone in the room. "You won't have to talk to strangers if you don't want to."

"Well, I don't want to, and there's almost no chance of it if I stay here."

"Some of them strangers might be real lookers," Charlie cut in. "I know you got an eye for a redhead when you see one."

Bear began to feel cornered. And that meant he could get dangerous. "Not that it's any of your business, people, but I get seasick. There. That's the end of it." He shut his mouth tight, not unlike Baby Benny when faced with a spoonful of medicine.

At that moment, Jessica breezed in and picked up the baby. "Thanks for watching him, Bear." She wrinkled her nose. "Hmmm. Smells like he needs a change."

"Yep. Goop to poop in next to no time."

"I'll see to it. Vinny's out front waiting for you all." The Cadillac could handle all five residents. "Frankie's already in the car."

"We'll talk more about it at the senior center," said Lily.

"Nothin' more to talk about. I'm not going." Bear stood, waited a couple seconds for his hips to stop barking, and *kachunked* on his quad cane out of the room. But he wasn't so far ahead that he didn't overhear the rest of them as he went out the door.

A crestfallen Eunice said, "He must know he can wear a patch for seasickness. Just behind his ear."

"It must be serious," said Charlie, unlocking the wheels of his chair and following the rest of the pack. "Redheads can usually bring him around."

✦ ✦ ✦

After a few hours of entertainment at the senior center, Vinny Tononi drove the group back home to Latin's Ranch. The Cadillac was approximately the same size as a cruise ship. Frankie, Eunice and Charlie sat in the back. Lily was sandwiched up front between Bear and Vinny.

Vinny was Frankie's bodyguard, chauffer and all around *goomba*. He was big, stern and often clanked with concealed weaponry. There was a time when he made Lily nervous. Now that he was her daughter's *amore*, Lily was edgier than ever. The high probability that one of them would end up broken hearted - or *cuore spezzato* depending - made her as jumpy as a jackrabbit.

Vinny took his eyes from the road long enough to look down at Lily. "You are well, Miss Lily? You are so quiet."

"Oh fine, fine. Just enjoying the spring color." Rhodies flashed by pink white pink white pink white as the vehicle zoomed toward home.

In fact, she wasn't fine. Their visit to the senior center had been unsatisfactory. First, she'd lost to a newcomer at Scrabble. That simply wouldn't do, and she needed a rematch soon. Then she'd made an effort to talk with Bear while he and Frankie checked and checkmated each other. But the big man wasn't talking about the cruise. She'd have to wait for a moment alone with him to find out the skinny.

CHAPTER ONE

Seasick?

That was bullshit and she just knew it.

They were approaching the Latin's Ranch driveway when Bear's phone rang. He frisked himself before locating the little device in a shirt pocket.

"What?" he asked into it when he found it. "No, we're gone ... no, I didn't ... no ... yeah. I think you maybe should stop by."

Bear clicked off. Lily watched him cloud over like a front moving in. She waited. Finally, she couldn't take it anymore. "Who was that? What's happened?"

"Someone was shot at the senior center right after we left. Cupcake's coming to talk about it." He turned his great head toward the back seat. "Eunice?"

"Bear?"

"Think I might go to Alaska with you after all."

CHAPTER TWO

Case Notes
May 3, 9 p.m.

Deputy Detective Josephine Keegan of the Major Crimes Unit stopped by at about six o'clock. Jo is a special favorite of all the Latin's Ranch gang ever since we worked that missing person case together. She's pretty good at telling us whether we're being helpful or buttinskies without hurting our feelings. It's a gift.
Bear knew her as a rookie sheriff's deputy long before he hung up his holster as a private investigator. He calls her Cupcake from back in the day. She hates it now, and I imagine she hated it then. But it's hard for an old Bear to change his stripes especially if he doesn't want to. Jo is a handsome woman but maybe a little less so than she used to be. After the painful fiasco with her partner Clay, she's become a sadder but wiser cupcake. You can see it in the set of her jaw and the wispy lines beginning to show around her eyes. More defensive, less likely to smile. Her dark hair is pulled straight back in a tight knot without one strand daring to misbehave. And I have to say, she's overly tough on her partners now. Snappish. I imagine the boys in the department call her a bitch. No. I imagine they call her worse than that.
I think she's on partner number three since Clay. This one must be scared of her. At least when she told him to stay outside, he nodded, muttered "Ma'am," and stayed. He sat on the porch while Furball

CHAPTER TWO

> *explored the overall suitability of his lap for a cat nap. That cat lays claim to all comfort zones before Jessica's dog, Folly, even has a chance.*
>
> *Bear pissed me off when he said he'd see Jo alone, meaning without me, his eWatson. How the hell can I keep the case notes if he keeps the case to himself? So I decided while the big man got the story from Jo, I'd take a run at the partner.*
>
> *I started my investigation with a plate of our cook Aurora's biscochitos. Even a hard-boiled cop would spill his guts for a couple of those cinnamon sugar cookies. And this guy was so far from hard-boiled he'd be child's play to crack.*
>
> *- Lily Gilbert, Investigative Assistant to PI Bear Jacobs*

Lily put on her sweet face and approached the target. "Hello, young man. My name is Lily Gilbert. I thought you might like a bit of refreshment while you wait out here." She set the plate of cookies on the little wicker occasional table beside his chair. Then she sat on the glider next to it and smiled broadly at the plump twenty-something officer.

He touched his hat brim. "Ma'am," he said.

Lily wondered if *ma'am* was the only word he knew. It was the only one she'd heard him say to Jo Keegan. Maybe he was merely shy. "And who might you be, young man?" she prompted.

"Deputy Detective Brandon Orwell at your service." He made a move to stand politely, but Furball hissed and extended a fistful of threatening claws in the direction of his crotch. Detective Orwell sat back down with extreme haste.

Lily decided he might be shy but he wasn't stupid. As he kept an eye on the fat orange cat, she said, "I'm the assistant to the private investigator that your partner is here to consult."

"A PI lives here?" He looked around quizzically at the farm house, the pastures, the barn. Nothing could look more bucolic. "My partner wants to consult with a PI?"

"Yes to both your questions."

He pursed his lips just a bit. Lily assumed he was grappling with Law Officer Conviction Number One, that official detectives never consult unofficial detectives.

"I know it is rare. But you see, this one was her mentor. Taught her everything she knows."

"Really? She knows a lot."

Clearly he believed Jo was not merely a ball buster but a knowledgeable one.

"Take a cookie, my dear. Enjoy while you have a brief break from your important duties. Now then, my friend Jo had a few things she wanted me to ask you while she talks to PI Jacobs."

"She did?" He took a bite of heaven and began to melt. "Wow, that's good."

"Have another." Pushing drugs couldn't be easier. "She asked that you give me your overall impression of what happened. You know, your take. Important to have an expert opinion before it is contaminated by others."

"Really? She called mine an expert opinion?" He actually beamed.

"Something very much like that. The exact words escape me. My memory isn't what it used to be, you see. But I am sure that was the sense of it. So, what time did the incident occur?"

"Well it must have happened between three and four pm, although forensics will have to confirm."

"Just tell me in your own words."

"An old lady bought it. Er, I mean a senior citizen was found deceased."

Now that he was talking, Lily had no intention of letting him stop. "Inside the senior center?"

"In their parking lot. Between two parked cars."

"How did she die?"

"Strangled is how it looked to me."

"Strangled?" Lily was surprised. Of course, no bullet meant no sound. "Did she scream? What was the weapon? A rope? A wire? Approached from behind? In front?"

"Behind. Strangled with a scarf. Nobody has reported hearing anything but we've just begun to interview -"

"A scarf? One of her own?"

CHAPTER TWO

Hadn't it been too warm for a scarf? Well except for the one that ...

"Yes, ma'am. A big square one. People saw her with it over her shoulders earlier in the day."

"A thin scarf like silk? Or heavy like wool?" In Lily's stomach butterflies were upping the game from flutter to thrash.

"Thin, ma'am. Bright red with a -"

The front door swung open. Detective Keegan came out, followed by Bear. Keegan barked, "Brandon!"

This time, the young man leaped up spilling Furball to the ground. The cat left a long scratch on his arm as it landed on its feet, lifted its tail and swayed away.

"Brandon, have you been yapping to this sweet little lady?"

"She said -"

"You've been played, kid. By an old woman with more curiosity than that cat. The scratch serves you right."

Lily continued playing the hostess. "I'll get a couple bandages, young man." Turning to the detective she said, "Care for some sugar cookies, Jo?"

"Thanks but no thanks, Miss Lily. Things are syrupy enough around here as is. And I have bandages in the cruiser. We'll just be on our way."

"Well, okay then, officers. Nice to meet you, Brandon."

He touched his hat once again. "Ma'am."

Bear *kachunked* on his cane over to the glider and sat next to Lily. As they watched the deputies depart in their cruiser, he hummed *Let's Go On a Sentimental Journey*.

Lily knew that he hummed when he was thinking. When the cruiser's dust in the drive had settled, he said to her, "You're worried."

She didn't answer.

"And you're pissed at me."

"Yes. Worried and pissed in equal measure."

"That's why I wanted to talk to Cupcake alone. No reason to worry you if this had nothing to do with Eunice. It would have worked if it weren't for Officer Spill The Beans." "So you knew about the red scarf?" She gave some thought to being mad at him for withholding information, but decided she'd rather listen than argue. At least this one time.

"When Jo called me, she mentioned it. And I saw the woman wearing it earlier myself. The scarf looked a lot like the one Eunice had on. Bright red with a pattern. Not birds maybe, but easy to confuse from a distance if the perp didn't know the victim personally."

"You think some stranger meant to kill Eunice?"

"Don't know. Probably not. My guess is a random attack. But it's not a bad time to sail away. Get her out of the area."

Lily knew Bear wasn't crazy about admitting he might be worried, too. But his next statement was a confession to just that. "Get you away, too, since you'd protect her. If she's in danger, you're in danger."

Lily drew a breath, held and expelled it. "It can't be about Eunice. Who the hell would want to hurt her other than the fashion police?"

"Nobody. Probably."

"I don't want to scare her, Bear. She's having such fun planning this trip."

"Then we won't tell her our suspicions. Just keep our eyes open until we're underway. I meant it when I said I'm going, too."

"Probably shouldn't tell Frankie either or the mob will overrun the ranch."

Bear snorted in agreement. "Last time that happened, Jessica used some damn colorful words for me."

They sat and glided for a while in companionable silence listening to the squeak of the metal accompany the song of a Western tanager. Then he added, "Keegan may have to talk with Eunice, but she'll be discreet. Or leave it up to me."

"You? Discreet?"

Lily could tell he was gathering steam to lecture her about his level of prudence vs hers when the front door opened again. Their youngest aide, Alita Aarons, leaned out and chirped, "There you are! Time for dinner you two. From the aroma of the *arroz con pollo*, I'd say Aurora has outdone herself again."

CHAPTER TWO

✦ ✦ ✦

It was a full house for dinner with all five residents, Vinny, Sam Hart the barn manager, Jessica, Ben and Baby Benny. Aurora and Alita served the *arroz con pollo* along with an avocado salad and crusty rolls. Many appreciative noises were made, but the death of the unknown woman was the real buzz.

"You go to a place as safe as a senior center and what happens? A murder, that's what!" Jessica shook her head causing her curls to dance. She looked up at the man who had been her husband for less than three months and rolled her beautiful blue eyes dramatically. "I can't turn my back on them, not for a minute."

Bennett Stassen was not only Jessica's new husband but the baby's natural grandfather as well as adoptive father. Everyone at the table knew he was consumed with doing all jobs well. At the moment he was engaged in another skirmish with Baby Benny regarding food intake. This one was over mashed carrots. By the looks of the highchair, floor and Ben's shirt, Baby Benny was winning. Grandpa Dad said, "Can't talk now, Jess. I'll get the hang of this if I concentrate."

"Besides, it wasn't one of us, Jess," Charlie said regarding the senior center murder. "We're all okay. So what's the worry?"

"Who was it, Bear? The deceased?" Jessica asked.

The group turned toward him. "Don't know. Hadn't seen her before today. According to Cupcake, her I.D. says she's from Idaho. Apparently visiting friends in the area."

He helped himself to a second serving of chicken as Eunice asked, "Why did Detective Keegan come talk to you?"

"Oh, just because we go to the senior center so often. You know, familiar with the scene of the crime and all. Might give her a few helpful hints." It didn't sound very believable even to Bear, but Lily helped him out by changing the subject.

"What will you be doing while we're on the cruise, Jessica?"

"We'll be on vacation here, of course, without you guys around to pester us. Sleep late, sit around and relax, romantic dinners ..."

Baby Benny had had enough and wailed like a fire siren. Ben got up to clean him up.

"Use the horse trough in the pasture. Big enough to dunk yourself, too," Sam called after him.

"You better send the kid with us if you hope for peace and quiet," Bear said to Jessica. "He'd fit in my duffle."

"Don't tempt me. Now then. I have all your birth certificates in a file for you." As the owner of Latin's Ranch, Jessica held most of their records. "Good idea to take a passport if you have one. If not, since the ship goes and comes from the same port, your driver's license should be okay."

Bear smiled to himself as Jessica tried to appear stern. Her curls, freckles and big blue eyes weren't the stuff of strictness. "But I don't want any of you driving, is that clear? In fact, nothing dangerous. Promise?"

"Except maybe that helicopter excursion over the fjords," said Bear.

"The dog sleds on Mendenhall Glacier," said Eunice.

"The zip line in Icy Point," said Frankie although in a Sicilian accent it sounded more like zeep line.

"The trek through grizzly country," said Lily.

"Shooting in a small boat the rapids," said Vinnie also accent-challenged.

"A shipboard romance," said Charlie while playing the air violin.

Jessica held up her hands like a traffic cop. "Knock it off all of you, or I won't take you to the dock on departure day."

By the time Aurora served coffee spiked with cinnamon and clove -- along with a dollop of vanilla ice cream or shot of tequila for those who wanted it -- the conversation had devolved to the subject of packing. Bear figured his duffle would work for him. But Eunice was going to need at least three mega-bags. And they had a small herd of mobility equipment from wheelchairs to canes.

The only device they'd leave behind was Sitting Bull, their customized golf cart. So they better have no need for quick escapes. Of course, why would they need something like that on a luxury cruise?

CHAPTER TWO

✦ ✦ ✦

Rick Peters thought he was keeping the lid on his secret. But he was over the moon, round the bend, beside himself with excitement. And everyone knew it.

Eunice had invited him on the cruise. He was to share an onboard suite with Bear and Charlie, continuing his usual duties as a Certified Nursing Assistant. But he'd have lots of free time, too, since the cruise staff was geared to passenger care. Besides, the old guys were pretty independent between the morning and evening changing and washing.

"Can you do a two-step? Have a tuxedo for formal night? Pretty good at bingo? Shuffleboard on deck?" Chrissie teased. The two aides were working together, putting fresh sheets on all the resident beds.

"Ah, you're just jealous, Chrissie. Imagine! A free cruise through the nation's best scenery." They'd been friends a long time so sniping came easily between them.

"Yeah, like you're interested in any scenery that doesn't involve boobs."

Rick looked stricken. "This is about my history, woman. My history." He was part Alutiiq. His ancestors from the Aleutian Islands had been treated like slaves by the early Russians who came to Kodiak to establish a fur trade in the eighteen hundreds. At some point, a trader had actually married a native princess. This female ancestor five times removed became a Petrov. Decades ago, the name had been Americanized to Peters. "I haven't been back home for years. The ship stops at Kodiak. I can't wait to see it again. Maybe find some long lost family."

"Uh-huh. I'm sure that's what has your tail in a twist." Chrissie said as Rick removed a bottom sheet. "Lucky for you I can't go what with two little ones at home." She snapped a fresh sheet into place. "Created an opportunity for Alita. You owe me, mister."

"You would have been my first choice, Chrissie. You're my BFF." It was bullshit told to a friend who knew better. The fact that Alita was going to care for Lily and Eunice was sensational news for Rick. He adored the girl, had for what seemed to a young man like ages. He would purchase a ring of Alaskan gold in Ketchikan or Juneau. And he'd ask her to marry him. It would be wonderful.

Chrissie stopped unfolding the next sheet and stared at him. "You moron. Do you really think I don't know you and Alita need a fire hose turned on you about half the time?"

He shushed her. "Maybe you know. But everyone else thinks I'm just playing around. Like usual."

"Hate to disappoint you, jackass, but your secret is out. You suck at subterfuge."

"No way!"

"We even have a pool on when you're popping the question."

Rick felt stunned. "Everyone knows?"

"Well, let's see ... staff, residents, management ..." She looked momentarily deep in thought. "Ah! I don't think Alita is in on it."

Six pillows hit her before she managed to get out the door.

CHAPTER THREE

Case Notes
May 10, 2 p.m.

A couple days ago, Jessica had a nurse come give us pneumonia shots plus tetanus boosters for any who needed one. She says it's a wise idea for all old farts (she didn't actually say farts), but I'm pretty sure it's because we're sailing away from her eagle eye. She's convinced we'll come to disaster. Good thing Alaska isn't known for malaria or dangue fever or we'd all feel like pin cushions. The nurse also left motion sickness patches to give to Bear. Speaking of Bear. He has a stiletto hidden inside his customized quad cane. It's mostly a joke, but it saved his bacon one night not that long ago. Yesterday he gave me a cane of my own. Except twist the handle on mine and you have a stun gun inside.

"An unusual gift, Bear," I said somewhat taken aback. "But a beautiful one." And it is, a cane made from oak burl wood.

"I chose a stun gun because I knew you weren't likely to use a knife."

"How thoughtful. Who knew you could get such a thing!"

"You could probably get one with a crossbow inside if you shopped long enough."

"Imagine."

"I ordered it when you got your new leg and was saving it for your birthday. But I decided you might need it on this cruise. Just in case you get attacked by a caribou. Or someone gets too interested in Eunice."

Okay, now the gumball dropped through my mechanism. "Ah. For protection. But, Bear, how the hell are you going to get your knife onboard?"

"Knives are okay."

"Knives are okay?"

"Well, little ones."

"Bear your stiletto is not little."

"Sure it is. In the cutlery world, lots are bigger. Bowie knives, machetes, ballock daggers ..."

"Ballock daggers?"

"Yep. Two oval swellings at the knife guard resemble -"

" I get the idea."

"I'll put my knife in my luggage so there's no issue at check in. Worst case scenario? They'll take it and give it back to me after the cruise. Satisfied?"

Weaponry is not my forte. If I had to protect Eunice with a knife, I'd need to ask the attacker to hold on a minute while I twisted open the cane, pulled out the blade and steadied myself for a throw, then ask him to walk in front of it. That's still better than the stun gun option. The cane tip is the stunny part and the handle is like a trigger. In an emergency, I'll probably activate it and deaden my one good leg. But I guess it's the thought that counts, and it pleases me that Bear thought of me, strange though his thought may be.

On the subject of weaponry, I wondered something else. "How will Vinny get his arsenal aboard?"

"He won't."

"No bazookas? Brass knuckles? Battle axes?"

"Nope. For most occasions, his own two fists are all the missiles he needs. Besides, Frankie will no doubt have alternative plans if necessary."

"Like what?"

"I don't want to know."

Me either, I guess, although I imagined a pod of killer whales leaping aboard to chow down on the enemy.

Bear, Charlie and Rick have one suite, Eunice, Alita and I have one,

CHAPTER THREE

and Frankie and Vinny have a third. Frankie didn't allow his little dove to pay for his room since he didn't consider it an appropriate thing for a lady to do. Besides, he could purchase the whole damn ship if he wanted to. He could probably buy Alaska back for a jillion dollars more than the Louisiana Purchase. Call it the Retired Crime Kingpin Purchase. Or Frankie's Folly.

Anyhoo, we're going to be quite a caravan to the ship. Jessica will drive some of us to Seattle's Pier 66 in her old Camry. Chrissie will take a load, and Ben will come with Vinny and all the luggage. Maybe we should get a parade permit.

We leave tomorrow. We'll be busy today with last minute packing so we'll be tired. But I'm betting none of us will sleep tonight.

- Lily Gilbert, Excited Assistant to PI Bear Jacobs

Latin's Ranch boarded horses long before it boarded people. Jessica raised Paso Fino show stock, trained trail horses, and gave riding lessons. The ranch's name came from her champion sire, Latin Lover. It was Jessica's relationship as a caregiver to Lily that had started the idea of an adult care facility. Jessica had opened her home and her heart to five seniors, but the horse business was still the main enterprise of Latin's Ranch.

Lily liked it that way. She didn't feel like a shut-in as she had at a nursing home even though her health was still in the hands of others. When she went outside, there was something to see and do, like planters to tend, foals to love, living things to talk with and nurture. The place was about all of life, not just the end of it. She was part of the rhythm of this acreage in the foothills of the Cascades.

"You always drive," she said to Bear as she sat next to him in Sitting Bull.

"I maintain many gender stereotypes," he said and zoomed away, if a golf cart could be said to zoom.

Lily wanted to ride around the ranch on the last afternoon before they left for Alaska. Sitting Bull was their method of transportation on the property and occasionally into town when Jessica wasn't around to question their shenanigans. The cart was customized to carry as many as four of the residents with their mobility equipment. They'd never needed space for all five since all five of them had never felt good enough at the same time to go anywhere. Such is life for old people.

"Kind of a shame to leave here right now. We wait a long bleak winter for all this color." Lily loved to putt slowly along the edge of the woods looking for wildflowers under the rhodies and flowering dogwoods. Bear had finally learned to go slow enough so she could peer at the violets, bitterroot and fairyslippers. It didn't exactly bore him, but his attitude was pretty much a rose was a rose was a rose. Since Lily had pointed out that a really good investigator would be a lot more observant than that, Bear had stopped griping about it.

"Oh! Before I forget," Lily said, reaching into the pocket of her cardigan. "Here. From the nurse. Put this on when we leave tomorrow."

"A condom?" he asked, looking at the little paper packet.

"No, idiot. A seasick patch. You wear it behind an ear."

"Ridiculous."

"We'll see when the ocean swells rival tsunamis."

"Bah. How do I know I need it?"

"Well, you could give it a go without it if you want to take your chances. They say the Alaska cruise is a good trainee cruise since the Inside Passage is usually pretty smooth and you get to a new port almost every day."

"My last trainee cruise took thousands of us to Nam in the comfort of prisoners of war."

"Wear the patch. It might help you create better memories this time around." As they putted up the drive, she changed the subject. "Let's go into the barn."

"Thought you wanted to circle the pasture."

"I maintain many gender stereotypes. A woman has the right to change her mind."

Bear drove Sitting Bull into the barn so Lily could say good-bye to the horses. He went stall to stall while she handed out slices of apple and touched several velvety soft muzzles. Afterwards he stopped the cart, saying he needed to place a call to Detective Keegan. He patted himself down looking for the pocket where he'd put the phone this time.

CHAPTER THREE

When he extracted it, Lily said, "Put it on speaker so I can hear, too."

"You think I'm a wizard with this thing? I barely know how to dial the damn number." He poked a button or two. "There."

"Hello?" said Detective Keegan.

"We leave tomorrow," Bear blurted as her voice blared through the speaker.

"Hello to you, too."

"Yeah, yeah. Wondered if you had any updates you could share."

"You don't have to yell, Bear," said Lily. "She can hear you."

"I can hear you, too, Lily," said the detective. "You ready to go?"

"Just about. I need to pack up my meds, then I'm done."

Bear growled. "Updates, for crying out loud. What about updates?"

"Not much new," Keegan said. "We interviewed everyone who was at the senior center around the time of the woman's death. Your gang had already left."

"Anyone see anything?"

"One old guy noticed a stranger running through the parking lot at the time in question. He's nearly deaf so if the victim made any noise short of a foghorn, he wouldn't have heard her."

"Could he at least describe the stranger?" Lily asked.

"Called him a hawk-nosed white guy. Said he only remembers the hawk thing because he thought it was funny."

"The nose was funny?"

"He said the guy was wearing a Twelfth Man jersey. Seahawks made him think of hawk-nosed. Get it?"

Bear said, "So you just have to find a Twelve in Seattle with a good sized honker."

"Yeah. No worries, right? Too bad I'm such a slacker or this case would have been closed days ago. Why don't you call me from your first port of call, assuming you can pull yourselves away from the buffet."

"No problem, Cupcake. This is Bear and Lily. Out."

"Bear?" Keegan called just before he disconnected.

"Yeah?"

"Don't call me Cupcake."

✦ ✦ ✦

Romance around Latin's Ranch was getting to be business as usual. There was the *will-she-say-yes-and-when* pool regarding Rick and Alita, as well as the flirtation between the two octogenarians, Eunice and Frankie. Jessica and Ben had married in the early winter, putting the sorrows of their past aside as the joys of their present blossomed along with the glorious Washington spring.

All this lovey-dovey crap did nothing to improve Sylvia Henderson's mood. Her own relationship had hit, if not the end of the line, then at least a major roadblock. She had never discussed her Christmas in California with anyone. Not her mother Lily, to be sure. Not even her friend Tony Sapienza.

"Come on, Syl," Tony pestered over a four-adjective coffee at Starbuck's. "Did you and the Italian stallion do the deed or not?"

"What happens in Disneyland stays in Disneyland," she'd answered then turned a metaphorical key at her lips.

In truth, nothing had happened in Disneyland at least as far as a tryst with Vinny went. She'd planned the trip with the hunk of hotness and his nephews, using the little brats as subterfuge to get Uncle Vin away from Latin's Ranch for a long weekend. She'd bought tasteful but sensual lingerie at My Fair Pair. She'd upgraded to a two-bedroom suite so the kiddos would be out of the way in a room of their own.

But one of them (she never did get their names straight) had gotten sick on California Screamin'. Probably she shouldn't have allowed the chocolate chip sundae after the chili dog and fried pickles, but then what did she know about urchins and their tummies? The kid had spent the night retching over the toilet with her holding his head and refraining from shrieking. Turns out Italian stallions aren't all that good with sick kids. Vinny hunkered in the other room with the spawn who remained well. It had been a miserable night.

Bottom line, her virtue was intact. No woman is at her best when speckled with vomit.

Damn it all.

CHAPTER THREE

Sylvia had never felt passion like this before. She'd always been a woman in control, a sophisticate with an eye for the rightness of things. Subdued, well-ordered rooms vs bright lived-in clutter. She'd known love before, but she wondered now if she'd ever known lust. Her husband, rest his soul, had been gay. Their love making had been infrequent and sweet. *But passionate?Meh.*

The first time she'd laid eyes on Vinny she'd wanted to be laid *by* Vinny. Her inner workings burst into boisterous activity like never before. Unmentionable private parts engorged and tingled and thrummed. She figured her eyes bugged out of their sockets like a cartoon character whose libido had run amok. The only words she could think of at the time were smutty phrases she'd never said aloud before.

But this man, this Vinny -- mobster though he may be -- wanted a caring relationship that was far more than the affairs of his past. She wanted heat, he offered sweet. Marriage was his goal. He wouldn't violate -- his word, not hers -- her without a wedding.

Damn it all to hell!

He made love to her with affection and kisses and kindness, but he wouldn't have sex with her. She was a lady, not to be trifled with like all the women of his past.

I want to bed him, not wed him!

Sylvia ached for the kind of action in her mother's secret stash of bodice rippers. She did her best to reason with Vinny without sounding desperate as a Siamese cat in heat. "You know I've been married, right? I'm not a dewy eyed young thing. I know what I'm doing."

"You are not like other women I have known. You must be cherished."

She'd seen *The Sopranos*. She knew the type of *goomahs* Vinny had most likely known. And she was different, at least in terms of wardrobe. *But still.*

"Maybe you won't like what's in store ... maybe you should check out the merchandise first." She made a hand and arm gesture that was meant to indicate her body although someone might have interpreted it as modern dance. Part of their problem, according to her friend Tony, was Vinny's iffy grasp of English and her reserve as far as calling a spade a spade.

But communication wasn't the problem this time. Vinny had shaken his head and touched her gently on the cheek. "Is not possible I will not like this store. This store is a chapel where I wish to worship."

Sylvia sighed and went back to the pediatrician's office that she was designing on her computer. Now Vinny was leaving for a couple weeks. Maybe that was a good thing. Maybe distance would make his heart grow fonder. Although the heart wasn't the body part she was actually thinking about.

She left the desk in her home office, went upstairs to her bedroom, removed her clothes and put on the My Fair Pair lingerie. She redressed then went back to work. She could enjoy the feel of the silky little bits of naughtiness even if her stallion chose not to.

✦ ✦ ✦

"You will simply have to take something out," Lily said. It was late afternoon and Eunice had just finished her packing. The two friends sat side by side on Eunice's bulging suitcase. It was on the bed, fat as a walrus in the sun, and they were bouncing up and down on it. It would not close.

"I don't see how I can take anything out. This is my dressy stuff for the ceremony in Juneau plus the four formal nights on shipboard. That's five evening gowns and five pairs of shoes and purses and evening jackets and … oh! my gosh, I've forgotten my ivory bustier."

Lily could see bits of satin and lace trying to escape the suitcase. "Ah, Eunice. This is Alaska. Don't you think formal night will be jeans without holes at the knees?"

"My casuals are in those bags there. One can never be too well appointed, Lily. Besides I own all this stuff and I'm damn well going to wear it again before I die." Eunice began to spring up and down once more.

"We're gonna need reinforcements." Lily pulled the call cord and Rick soon appeared.

He stopped at the door and laughed at the bouncing duet. "You two playing Whac-a-Mole?"

"Try as we might we can't get this closed." Bounce, bounce.

CHAPTER THREE

"Let me help. Just stand back."

They got off the suitcase and out of the way. He thrashed, pushed and wrestled. Punched, shoved and heaved. Eventually he called Chrissie. Between the two of them they finally muscled it shut then buckled a luggage strap around it. And a second one.

"For the love of God," Chrissie said pushing the hair out of her eyes and gulping down air. "Jump back when you open it. It's sure to explode. Warn Alita. Warn the ship captain."

Lily imagined a ship cabin shrapneled with glitter. She pointed out the open cases in the corner of the room. "There're three more bags to go if you want to come back after dinner," she said to the aides.

✦ ✦ ✦

"Gonna find us a couple of babes on board," Charlie enthused as he emptied his underwear drawer into a suitcase that was old when Samsonite came to be. The willowy septuagenarian looked a bit like a wheelchair-bound basset hound, complete with deep soft jowls. He would have been handsome in a comical sort of way if he didn't insist on the comb-over that did more to heighten than hide baldness. "Babes with bucks, and I don't mean the kind with antlers. Although it's okay by me if they're horny. Ha!"

Bear would gag but that would just egg Charlie on. He settled for curling a lip, but Charlie ignore it.

Charlie was the most physically fragile of them all. He suffered sores on his scrotum, not an uncommon ailment for wheelchair jocks. A home health nurse came twice a week to administer care in that very private area. To survive the two week trip, she had provided him with a prescription cream he could self administer. It was a temporary fix. Otherwise, he would not have been able to go.

"Have you packed that cream?" Bear asked.

"A man never forgets his nuts," Charlie answered. His voice, which should have been the deep bay of a hound on the hunt, was actually high, almost girlish. "Medicine was the first thing in the bag. Got another tube in my pocket for emergency use."

That's all Bear cared to know about that. He hummed *Happy Trails to You* and watched as his roommate packed his dopp kit, Old Spice cologne, and a book on Alaskan history.

Charlie was the most mentally fragile of them all, too. He wasn't losing acuity, he'd just never had much of it. It was hard to imagine a situation that his brain power would plus. The fact of the matter was Charlie was not the easiest person to like. Bear had shared a room at the nursing home with him. When they moved to Latin's Ranch, Bear couldn't leave him behind. And Jessica needed the income from a full house to keep operating in the black. Over time, the Latin's Ranch group had grown accustomed to him. He was annoying, but he was theirs.

For his part, Charlie had stepped up to the plate. He did small handyman projects around the place for Jessica. He shared the comics with Eunice and was the only one of them who'd giggle with her about *Pickles*. He happened to be a pretty good baker, making forays into the kitchen in the middle of the night when Aurora wasn't there to stop him. His snickerdoodles were unparalleled in sweet deliciousness.

Besides, his womanizing bullshit was mostly bluff. Charlie's wife had stopped visiting him long before she was murdered in Bear's first case as a retired PI. Bear knew Charlie missed Louise and always would. Even a trained investigator such as himself couldn't figure out the mysteries of the heart.

"I have one suit," Charlie said, lifting a somber black number number out of the closet. "It's the suit I'm to be buried in. The one purchase that the Mrs. didn't resent making for me. Guess she was eager to see me in it. Who knew I'd outlast her?"

Bear's own packing was done. He saw no point in loading two weeks worth of stuff when laundry could be done on board. Besides, he didn't own two weeks worth of stuff.

He'd lost weight in long term care and even more at Latin's Ranch because of the better quality food and the upswing in his activity level. He wasn't as big as he once was, but his pants still were. So Bear had taken to wearing suspenders. Plain ones at first. Nothing fancy. Then subdued colors. Then wild patterns. He'd never admit to vanity but Lily called him on it.

"Suspenders have become a barometer to your moods," she'd announced at dinner one evening.

Whatever.

He'd tucked a variety of them into the duffle, then added his vintage plaid robe, a favorite hat, plus some other old reliables. Looking at the flaccid bag yesterday, even Bear knew it was too Spartan a collection. Shopping was mandatory.

Crap.

Lily would want to stick her nose in. Or even worse, Eunice. So Bear had Sam Hart take him to Goodwill where he splurged on a pair of pants, two flannel shirts, a cardigan and a North Face rain jacket that appeared to have never been worn. A pair of water proof boots, well broken in by some logger, had caught his eye. Bear wasn't up to much tree felling, but he liked the feeling of the boots, the independence that came with them. In Alaska, he would look like a local instead of a cruise wuss.

Well, maybe not.

After dinner, Bear *kachunked* to the patio door and out to Sitting Bull. He stared at it a moment then changed his mind. No time like the present to try out the new-to-him boots. He began the walk up the drive to Sam's trailer. It was the last evening of poker and cigars with his buddy for more than two weeks ... and the last evening he might actually enjoy until they came back home.

CHAPTER FOUR

Case Notes
May 11, 10 p.m.

Maybe in a few weeks this day will seem hilarious. But today? Horrendous. A major pile of crap.
Our ship is the Celestial Superstar. *According to her press, she's over nine hundred feet long and can carry 2,100 passengers plus nearly 800 crew members at a cruising speed of twenty-four knots. She makes the Alaska run all summer, round trip from Seattle. The ship docks here every couple of weeks early in the morning, unloads and reloads, then sets sail again around five in the afternoon.*
At least that's the theory. But today, our ship came in late. We arrived at the cruise terminal about the same time 2,100 incoming passengers were trying to get off the boat. Whatever good a vacation had done them was eradicated as they realized they would miss any connecting travel plans they had. They were a tidal wave of disgruntled flesh breaking over our crowd of fun seekers about to embark on the trip of a lifetime, eager to board and belly up to the buffet.
A couple thousand pissed off people vying for the same space as a couple thousand blissful people. Mad house does not describe this scene. Bedlam, maybe. Looney bin, nuttery, cuckoo's nest. If the term is politically correct it doesn't do justice to the occasion.
Another complication? It's early in the season so it should be cool. But it was one of those rare days in a Seattle spring when the city

CHAPTER FOUR

melts in the sun. Like everyone else, our gang was way overdressed. Speedos would have been a better choice. All the afore mentioned disgruntled people were hot disgruntled people.

We waited hours in the heat before boarding. All around us people threatened to sue, security officers hollered, cruise employees tried to placate. After the first two hours, ship staff came around to offer everyone water and snacks. About half the passengers informed them where they could put their cookies. Patience is not an American virtue.

People with mobility devices were herded together in a roped off community of the fragile, sort of like a leper colony. I thought it was for our protection until I saw how many of us 'fragile' people use motorized scooters, canes and wheelchairs as offensive weapons. The infirm were corralled to protect the firm, not the other way around. I felt like caning a young man myself when I overheard him say, "At least the gimps get to sit."

Once on board, we realized the free flute of 'welcome aboard' champagne would knock us on our exhausted keisters so we refused the libation. Frankie demanded we be shown to our cabins immediately. I believe he might have added 'or sleep with the fishes' but I can't swear to it. A sweet young man whose name seemed to be GIFHIGR showed us the way. Next time, I'll get close enough to read the badge.

I don't know about the rest of the gang, but Eunice and I each peeled off several layers then collapsed on our beds. She said something about never knowing just how much a person's feet could swell in the heat. I said I hadn't realized until that very day that scooters didn't have brakes. We thought we would be able to rest before dinner but we didn't get to stay still for long. That sweet young man whose name is a mystery? He rousted us. Said we had to get up immediately to go to the lifeboat drill.

"*Yeah? What if we don't?*" *Eunice, rarely argumentative, sounded pugnacious as a rabid weasel. Her charm bracelet clanged instead of tinkled.*

"*I will come looking for you, madam.*" *GIFHIGR was unflappable.*

"*What if I hide in the shower?*"

"*You cannot escape me, madam.*"

"*What are you gonna do to me?*"

"You will be keel hauled, madam."

I realized GIFHIGR's real name must be Stoolie.

Our aide Alita, a youngster who hates fusses, cut in. "I'll be sure they get to the drill. No worries."

Stoolie looked relieved to find a reasonable young person among the ruins. "I am so glad to see you eye to eye."

"Pardon?" Alita asked.

"He means he's glad you see eye to eye," I said, raising my old carcass off the bed. "On to the muster station."

It was worse than I thought it would be. After experiencing the drill on deck in a blistering hot sun jammed between dozens of strangers, I think that keel hauling might have been preferable. Ship personnel swear that, during an emergency, the crew will be there to save your butts vs. their own. That your fellow passengers will remain orderly during a fire at sea or an ice berg collision. But we'd just witnessed how everyone behaved when someone took cuts in line out on the dock. Nonetheless, we stared at the itty-bitty lifeboat that was to save our souls, and learned how to manipulate the life jackets. Probably the most dangerous time for the entire cruise was trying to huddle against a railing at the end of the drill when 2100 people headed for the elevators, all ripping off vests as though they were infested with lice.

When the coast was clear we returned to our rooms to await the arrival of our luggage. Meanwhile Rick and Alita were dispatched to find out why half of our group was booked for the early dinner seating and the other half for the late when our reservations had been confirmed for one time. At that moment I couldn't care less about dinner or luggage or how many whales might be at play in Puget Sound. Just before I fell asleep I heard Eunice say, "I hope I won't be sorry for getting us into this."

"Things will get better once we're under way," I answered. Then I didn't wake again until nightfall, my mouth dry from snoring and slobber congealed on my chin. And so our journey began.

- Lily Gilbert, Old Salt Assistant to PI Bear Jacobs

CHAPTER FOUR

Rick accompanied Bear to the dining room. Charlie was left behind with a room service menu. His luggage had still not been delivered to the room, and the outfit he was wearing included a t-shirt with the slogan *I'm Old. Go Around Me.* He thought this travel wear might be too casual for dinner even though it wasn't formal night.

The confusion over the seating time had been cleared away with the help of an assistant maitre d'. A circular table for eight was claimed by the Latin's Ranch gang for the six o'clock seating for the next two weeks. Alita and Vinny had already arrived and positioned themselves diagonally across from each other. Bear wondered if these two had ever actually said a word aloud to each other before. Apparently not. They both flashed joyful looks of relief at the arrival of Rick and Bear.

"Lily and Eunice are sleeping. I tried to wake them but Eunice called me an unpleasant name," Alita said.

Vinny added, "My *padrone*, he sleep too. He do worse than call me name if I wake him."

Was Vinny actually making a joke?

"Charlie isn't coming either," Bear said taking a seat. Or trying to. He tugged on it. Then he gave it a great pull. Slowly it moved back from the table. "Damn chairs weigh a ton. They'd make it through a cyclone without tipping over."

"Or a bout with the Kraken," Rick added as he wrestled his own chair into position. When he finished, he was tucked up as close to Alita as he could decently get.

A waiter, assistant waiter, head waiter, sommelier and bar man stopped by to introduce themselves and be of service. All were so friendly it was as though they were auditioning for the role of everyone's BFFs.

"Good thing Aurora isn't here. She'd want a big staff like this," Alita said. Dimples appeared when she laughed. "And did you meet our room steward, Alejandro? What a sweet guy. He brought ice and towels and said to call him if we need anything else and that he was sure the ladies would feel better tomorrow. I hope so."

Bear figured Rick would be one lucky dude if this girl said yes at proposal time. Even accepting that all old people think all young people are cute, this one was the very definition of the word. Her eyes sparkled with hope and promise, her skin was rose petal perfect. With enough Alitas in the world, maybe it wouldn't go down a rat hole. Her very presence lightened Bear's mood. This was unseemly for an avowed curmudgeon. He looked down at a menu and asked, "What the hell is *cacio e pepe?*"

In an unprecedented turn of events, Vinny was able to translate a document for the others. "Ez spaghetti, Signore Bear."

Eventually, orders were placed and drinks arrived. Bear looked around at the other diners in the room. Hundreds of them. He was aware of battles over seating choices. But mostly, strangers were greeting each other with excitement and anticipation of good times ahead. Somewhere between dock and dining, the crowd had turned happy. It didn't look like a riot would happen any time soon.

"What you looking for Bear?" Rick asked. "You're frowning."

"I'm looking for a hawk-nosed man."

They were interrupted as appetizers were served. Crab arancini, beef carpaccio, crispy calamari, kalamata bruschetta. Bear stared at the plates as they were doled out. He could only recognize two out of four but thought they all looked good enough to eat. The whole dining room filled with the aromas of baked goods, grilled meats, spiced vegetables.

"What is hawk nose? Es a beak?" asked Vinny, clearly enjoying the breaded squid.

"Sort of. A beezer with a prominent bridge that bends downward." Bear took a bite of the olive tapanade. "Damn tasty olives."

"Why are you looking for men with big noses, Bear?" Alita asked.

She hadn't been at the table the night he'd told the others. Bear explained. "You know a woman was killed the last day we were at the senior center."

"Right," said Rick through a mouthful of bruschetta covered in grilled cheese.

"A witness saw a hawk-nosed man run through the parking lot at about the time of the death."

"A stranger, I take it," Alita said then added, "This crab is delicious."

"But why would Hawk Nose be here?" Rick asked.

"Probably wouldn't. But the dead woman was wearing a shawl like the one Eunice had on that day. Lily and I have wondered if the victim might

CHAPTER FOUR

be a mistaken identity. Just a thought, nothing for sure."

"You mean someone might be after Eunice?" Alita paled and set down her fork. "And he might have followed us on board? Not cool!"

"I doubt he's here. But Lily and I are keeping our eyes open. Just in case. We haven't told Eunice because we don't want her to worry."

"My *padrone*. He knows this?"

"No. I saw no reason to alarm him either. Let them have fun. But I thought maybe you three could be on the alert for anything out of the usual."

A selection of Caesar, beet, goat cheese and artichoke salads was served.

"This food is out of the usual," Rick observed. He picked at a mystery green with a fork.

"*Signore* Bear, you have seen a Hawk Nose on this ship?" Vinny asked, looking prepared to attack the bastard with a butter knife.

"Yeah. About two hundred of them. And that's just among the passengers."

✦ ✦ ✦

By the next morning, Lily and Eunice were rested and excited about the days ahead. They'd met Alejandro who'd brought them fresh fruit and flowers, provided them with fluffy terry robes, opened their drapes to a fabulous view of the Pacific, and regaled them with ship gossip about people they didn't even know. When their room service breakfast had arrived, he arranged it on the suite's dining table and served them like traveling royalty.

Now they were relaxing in the Panorama Lounge at the top of the ship with a 180 degree view of the Pacific. Today, the ocean was neither Kipling's old grey widow maker nor the happy bounding main of the children's song. It's mood was somewhere in between, as though it were deciding between smooth sailing and hissy fits. Lily could see no land in any direction and for the first time thought that this enormous ship was rather miniscule in the face of all that water power.

As the ocean rolled in multiple shades of green and blue, it lulled away her aches and stress. She realized that the purpose of the first full day of a cruise was to recover from getting to the cruise. In the days ahead, there would be so many exotic stops. Like Juneau, the only state capital with no roads in or out. The fabled gold rush gateway of Skagway. The island of Kodiak where bears by the same name still lived free. So many ports with shopping, sightseeing, exploring. But today? Today was all about relaxation.

"How about a full body wax? Or a seaweed leaf wrap?" Eunice read aloud from the menu of spa services. Frankie looked at her as though he wished he understood this strange new language his little dove was cooing.

"I believe I'll go for the energizing body glow following a paraffin feet treatment. Maybe I'll get a discount since I only have one foot." Lily found the list of spa treatments very entertaining.

Bear perused a *Celestial Stargazer*, the ship's daily program of activities. "Think I'll go to morning trivia then to the digital workshop on Photoshop. Maybe the naturalist lecture on whale migration this afternoon." He took off a battered pair of reading glasses, pulled a slipping suspender strap back into position, and said, "Eunice, this cruising thing isn't bad after all."

"Oh! Thank you Bear." Her smile was as dazzling as her tangerine top with its lighthouse outlined in rhinestones.

Lily knew how much Eunice wanted everyone to have a good time, and yesterday had not been a great start. How nice of Bear to actually show an interest. In fact, everyone seemed to be feeling chipper.

Sometime during the evening they had sailed by Victoria, British Columbia and then out the Strait of Juan de Fuca, past Cape Flattery and into the open ocean. Now the ship was cruising up the west side of Vancouver Island. Lily had seen dolphins rushing beside the ship like dogs chasing cars. Some passengers had spotted a humpback breech, but she had only seen the spout. What a thrill to know something so large could still exist in the vastness of the Pacific. She'd been told it could be very rough here on the open ocean where winds whipped up the waves. But today it was gentle, not affecting any of them with motion sickness. Lily thought she wouldn't mention the patch she saw behind Bear's ear.

Charlie was the only one of them who was not at peace with his environment. Rick had wheeled him away to go shopping because his suitcase was still missing. If it was found on the dock in Seattle it would be sent by

CHAPTER FOUR

air to meet them in Ketchikan or Juneau. In the meantime, Celestial had given him vouchers to buy a few necessities in the onboard shops.

"He didn't lose his, ah, his cream for his, ah ..." Lily asked Bear.

"For his nuts? One tube. But he had a spare in his jacket pocket," Bear answered.

"Where's the rest of our group?" Eunice asked as a waiter came around with a tray of delicate baked goods for a mid morning snack.

"Vinny es in the gym," said Frankie.

"Rick will probably join Alita for a couples massage when he brings Charlie back. Or they'll be off learning how to salsa with the ship's dancers."

"Did anyone get to the show last night?" Bear asked.

"Those two did. I didn't even hear Alita come in during the wee hours."

Bear left for his trivia game. Frankie dozed and Eunice pulled a project from her craft bag. She was completing a knitted jacket for Baby Benny and trying to figure how many brown beads she'd need to create a moose on its pouch. "I'll buy them in Ketchikan so it will be a real Alaska souvenir."

Lily didn't say that the beads in Ketchikan probably came from China. No need to be snarky while Eunice was having such fun.

"I think I'll get a few green ones, too, so my moose can wear a scarf."

Lily drifted and watched the water go by, nine decks below the lounge. Gulls wheeled around the ship but the thick glass windows silenced their raucous cries. Sometime this afternoon the *Superstar* would duck behind Canada's Queen Charlotte Islands and enter the Inside Passage on its way to Ketchikan. Captain George Vancouver had sailed up the passage more than two centuries ahead of the *Superstar*. The difference? His full-rigged survey ship *Discovery* was powered by wind and less than one hundred feet in length.

Guess we know who the real Superstar was.

If the winds were strong and blowing opposite high tide, the going could get rough at this southernmost entrance to the Passage. That was something else she felt no need to share aloud. Why create worry in advance?

Her thoughts left the distant past of the explorers and landed just last winter at Latin's Ranch. She had learned to get around with an artificial leg. Not that long ago, she'd been told she would never be strong enough.

Now here she was, a passenger on a luxury cruise. She could walk from her suite at one end all the way to the buffet at the other. Maybe not twice in a row without a rest, but she could do it. It was more proof that getting old didn't mean you had to roll over and play dead.

Next I'll be joining Vinny in the gym for a workout on the elliptical.

These people she lived with were dearer to her than any family she had ever known. Except for Sylvia, of course. Nobody could touch the place that her daughter held in her heart. But Eunice, Bear and the rest? She'd met them all after she'd landed in a nursing home. Together they had built a life that was an adventure of its own. It didn't replace the years before, of course. There was grief and always pain. But if you let yourself change and learn and explore? Then old age was a great deal more than a time to count up your losses.

Charlie wheeled himself into the lounge, interrupting Lily's reverie when he halted in front of her. Eunice looked up from her knitting and Frankie snorted where he slept, encased in an easy chair.

"Not a lot of choice in the Celestial shop," Charlie said. He was dressed like a parody of a cruiser. The bright red sweat pants had a vibrant pattern of seafaring signal flags. A long sleeved navy t-shirt emblazoned SUPERSTAR across his chest. Even his new socks had a pattern of entwined anchors.

"Hello, sailor," said Lily.

"Have you seen the great white whale?" Eunice asked, lifting her hand to her eyes and staring out at the horizon.

"Sure, make fun. But I know I'm lookin' good. The doll who sold me these duds told me so. Said most old guys didn't have the pizzazz."

Lily thought if the sales woman worked on commission, she'd just found an easy bird to pluck. But it was another snarky thought that didn't need to be said aloud.

Suppose this cruise is actually sweetening me up?

Throughout the day, they went to activities, sat on a deck until the chill drove them in, took long naps, exclaimed over the scenery. Lily occasionally passed one of the others in the hall on the way to bingo in one direction as she went to the deck sale or a card game in the other. The next time they were all together was at dinner that evening.

"Tomorrow we get to Ketchikan," Lily said, enjoying a warm piece of fresh baked bread along with her tortellini spinach soup. "I've been looking at the shore excursions. I'd like to see some of the totem poles. There are more in Ketchikan than anywhere else in the world."

"And I have shopping to do," Eunice chipped in.

"What the hell you buying in Ketchikan? You running low on soapstone carvings?" Bear asked.

"No, smarty. I need beads for the baby sweater. And a person just never knows what might jump into her shopping cart although probably not gifts for grumpy old poops." Eunice turned to Lily. "I booked us a private van. Didn't think we were up for a tour bus. It will take us sightseeing and shopping both."

"Perfect." Lily knew she could count on Eunice to be organized. It was a mistake to think she was a ditz just because she looked like one.

"Alita, you come with us, okay? Anyone else? Bear?"

"Been years since I went fishing. I have a yen to do a charter. Too early for halibut but good for king salmon."

"Think they can handle a guy in a wheelchair? I'd like to go, too," said Charlie. "Especially if afterwards we can go to that dance hall I've been hearing about."

"Even if we don't catch anything, we should see lots of eagles. Maybe humpbacks, too," Bear said before taking a bite of prime rib.

"I'll tag along to make sure neither of you falls overboard," Rick said. "Show you how a real fisherman works."

"What about the dance hall?" Charlie fretted.

"Okay," Bear said. "But you know there aren't any real Miss Kitties there anymore, right?"

"A man can dream."

"How about you, Vinny? Care to come along?" Bear asked.

"Vinny does important errand for me tomorrow," said Frankie.

That stopped the conversation. Lily wondered what kind of errand a retired crime boss could possibly have in Ketchikan. She'd never ask, but her curiosity lifted off like a rocket.

Checking up on the illegal halibut cheek trade? Running totems in salmon cans? Counting corpses that slept with the fishes?

"So you come with us, Frankie. There's lots of room in the van," Eunice asked, batting the few natural eyelashes she had left which were presently laden with Meet Me at Midnight mascara.

"No, my little dove. I stay on ship and await your return. Is safer that way."

Lily knew he avoided crowds. But she didn't think a bunch of tourists would rattle him. The old guy had something else in mind.

Now what do you suppose?

One thing about travelling with a crime boss, even a retired one. The Italian maitre d' had nearly gasped when Frankie first entered the dining room as the Latin's Ranch gang made the long slow procession to their table. As they laced between other tables on their canes, wheelchairs and walkers, a silent alarm spread from host to waiter to busboy. Ever since, nothing was too good for any of them. Free wine arrived. Smiles were even broader. Frankie's past could be scary, true, but there was an upside to traveling with a mobster.

CHAPTER FIVE

Case Notes
May 14, 2 a.m.

It's quiet now. Eunice and I are both in our beds, needing sleep but it won't happen. Sorrow steals your ability to turn off your brain. I keep playing the whole thing over and over in my head. I cannot conceive of the how and the why. But I'm getting ahead of myself. I need to start before the day went so wrong.
Our morning of Ketchikan sightseeing was lovely. It was cool and cloudy so the people on board from places like New Mexico or Florida were unhappy. But for us Northwesterners, liquid sunshine is business as usual. We have as many words for rain as native Alaskans have for snow.
We all had stories to share when we regrouped in the midship Take Five Bar this afternoon.
The men had seen orcas and sea lions on their fishing excursion as well as eagles. "No short-tailed albatross, I'm afraid," Bear said to Eunice. He sipped his Alaskan Stout then added, "But a lot of floatplanes so beat up it's hard to believe they still fly. The same is true of the bush pilots, too."
Rick had arranged to have the king salmon that he and Bear caught sent back to Aurora at Latin's Ranch. "We'll have great steaks for days once we get home," he said with pride.

Charlie's luggage was waiting for him in Ketchikan and delivered first thing to his room so he had a coat for the fishing excursion. His good luck continued when he met a woman at the dancehall who is a passenger on this ship. According to Bear, she really is a nice looking type who seemed friendly. Charlie's now over the moon with possibilities. He hopes to find her after dinner this evening. Knowing Charlie, he'll be snoring shortly after the dining room management clears us away with the crumbs in time for the second seating. I doubt that a relationship will flourish for Charlie unless the woman enjoys her romance during daylight hours.

Eunice, Alita and I liked our van driver, and much to our surprise, Vasily was actually a local. Not many live in Ketchikan year round since the summer tourist season is the town's bread and butter. Logging, canneries and commercial fishing aren't what they once were. It takes a hearty soul to put up with the wet, dark loneliness of the winters when sightseers stay far away. Vasily said our next port of call, Juneau, was different ... lots of people live there year round since it is the state capital. He called his cousin there to meet us with a vehicle, so we know we'll have good service in that port, too.

Today in May, Ketchikan bustled. Vasily showed us the sights then let us explore the tourist shops. Eunice found some adorable wooden beads carved like tiny moose and bears. Perfect for Baby Benny's sweater. While she strolled shop to shop, Alita and I chilled at a coffee bar. I can walk, but I can't keep up with Eunice when she sniffs a bargain in the wind.

Vinny was the last to arrive at the Take Five Bar and handed a tiny pouch to Frankie. It was no bigger than a coin purse and looked to be made from velvet. In Vinny's ham hock of a hand it appeared fragile as a butterfly.

"'E buono?" Frankie asked.

"'E buono," Vinny answered.

"And the other matter?"

"Es taken care of, my padrone."

Frankie nodded. Vinny took his arm and helped him stand. Frankie is the oldest of us, but it would be a mistake to think he is no longer a

CHAPTER FIVE

man with power. I know of a few who have doubted him who are not around to doubt anything again. The soft folds in his face rounded upward as he handed the pouch to Eunice with as much panache as an octogenarian can muster.

"For me?" Her face lit like a sunrise.

"Es for you, my little dove." Frankie executed a courtly bow. Vinny supported him then helped him back to his chair.

The little dove fluffed and cooed. She carefully opened the pouch and then an inner wrap that looked soft as lens cloth.

"Oh. Oh! OH MY!!" She held up a golden egg. It flashed and sparkled with inlayed gemstones. I don't know my eggs all that well, but I'd say this one looked like Fabergé.

"Ez more! Keep going," Frankie exclaimed. Eunice's obvious surprise was pure pleasure for the old don. His eyes sparkled damn near as much as the egg.

Eunice held her treasure close and discovered a tiny gold clasp. "Why, it's a jewel box!" She was as focused as our cat Furball when he's about to pounce. Slowly, she lifted the lid and revealed a brooch that made her gasp.

From where I sat, it looked to be white enamel with gold filigree in the shape of a beautiful flying bird.

"It's an albatross! Everyone, look." Her tone took on a certain reverence, and she handed the brooch to me to pass around. In my hands, I could see that the bird's eye was an emerald and the sparkle like dewdrops on the wings had to be diamonds. The body, surrounded by delicate enamel feathers outlined in gold, appeared to be an opal. Eunice has money and she has nice things. But I doubt even she has ever owned anything like this before.

While we passed the brooch from person to person as carefully as Communion wafers, Frankie told its story. "They say ez Russian antique brought to Alaska by man rich from furs." As the story went, the trader gave it to his wife in the late 1800s. But she died of small pox and the brooch disappeared soon after that. Frankie had hired an Alaskan estate broker to find something special for Eunice to commemorate her award from PASTA. This is what the agent found, described to Frankie and delivered to Ketchikan for Vinny to handle the payment and guard the bird back to the ship. It had been authenticated as genuine antique Russian handwork so it was real, even if its story was a fairy tale.

"Gorgeous," said Charlie and "Very special," said Alita. I'd say Rick looked at it sadly as he said, "Its family must miss it." I now wish I had paid more attention to him.

"It is stunning," Eunice said when the brooch migrated around the group and landed back in her hands. And it was. Maybe wrong for a young woman. Or a tailored one. But for my bigger-than-life old friend? It was the perfect gift.

"I will treasure it always." She stood and leaned down to kiss Frankie's cheek. His face did that upturned foldy thing again. "Tonight is formal night, and I will wear it with great pride. I'll go now and get ready." She left as regally as the Superstar did when it pulled away from its dock. Before long, we all trooped to our rooms like the handicapped troopers we are. Dinner would soon be served, and the evening festivities would begin and we'd all have a marvelous time.

If only it had ended that way.

- Lily Gilbert, Gussied Up Assistant to PI Bear Jacobs

When Lily arrived at her cabin, Alita was styling Eunice for the evening, and the two were fussing at each other.

"I don't tell you about birds. Now don't you tell me about hair." Alita had brushed out the spikes but Eunice's hair now stood out like a solid orange buzz cut.

"I look like a warning sign with its pole in a socket."

"Keep complaining and I might just leave it like this."

"How do I know it will get any better?'

"Because I love you, and I wouldn't let a loved one be seen in public looking like this."

Lily couldn't help but laugh. Eunice looked at her. "I ask you. When did our sweet Alita get so bossy?"

CHAPTER FIVE

"My guess? When she started hanging out with you. I mean us."

Alita applied a blob of gel. "Just be patient, Miss Eunice. The glitter is going to set off that hunk of bird rock you're wearing tonight." She popped the lid off a spray can. "It's called Moonlight Madness." Alita began spraying, alternating glitter with hairspray to keep it stuck on Eunice's head.

Lily escaped to the balcony before she passed out from fumes. She wrapped herself in a beach towel, watched the Ketchikan activity nine decks below, and breathed deep the scents of salt, sea and forest. She spied an eagle using sailboat beams as a perch. It swooped down on unsuspecting fish in the harbor then back up for another go.

Her own wardrobe for the evening would require far less fussing than Eunice so she had time to relax with her thoughts. Her top was an ivory tank with a deep v-neck. It was a peplum shape that cut in at her waist then flared out over her hips. The back had a crisscross tie from nape to mid back. Lily's bare arms were still well muscled from the exertion of walkers, and her waist was as narrow as when she was a girl. She knew she would look good if not as glammed as Eunice.

Her tuxedo pants were embellished with satin pinstripes down the sides. The pant legs were wide enough to accommodate her prosthetic. She remembered a time when dressing up hadn't included that particular problem. Lily shook her head as though warding off a wasp. No reason to dwell on loss.

The thought of her shoes trailed a smile across her face. As a one-legged lady, she usually opted for safe, serviceable footwear. Her real foot received more stress now while walking and needed a decent sole to absorb shock. But safe, serviceable shoes didn't have to be ugly. Did they?

Sylvia had taken Lily and Eunice to Nordstrom's on their quest to buy shoes for the trip. Shoes both practical and pretty.

"How about these?" Eunice had said, teetering around the shoe department in gladiator platform sandals as her ankles wobbled and she clung to one shoe display or another. "Remember that ships rock and roll," Sylvia said.

"Dangerous to be in spikes," Lily said.

"How could you dance in them when you can't even walk in them?" Sylvia added.

"Who'll get you to sick bay when you fall?"

Eunice put her hands on her hips. "So, I take it you don't like them? You two really need to watch more *Project Runway*. How shoes feel have nothing to do with how they look, you know."

Eventually, Eunice had settled on gold toned peep toe pumps with pleats across the vamp, dubbing them sizzling but sensible. And Lily had found lovely ivory flats. Tiny crystals twinkled in the embroidery that looked like lace across the toe. She would put a padded insert in the shoe that went on her real foot, but still feel like her feet were, in fact, pretty.

Goal accomplished.

It had been a long time since she'd thought of herself as pretty. "It appears I have not lost my vanity," she said to her daughter. "Thank you for taking this time. In fact, my dear, I don't thank you often enough. And thank you, Eunice for the gift of this trip. I never in my life thought I'd be able to travel again."

All three were sniveling by the time they left the store.

Tears threatened Lily again so she stood and left the cabin's private balcony. It was time for her to dress for dinner. When she entered the cabin and saw Eunice, it stopped her in her tracks. "Wow," she said. "I mean ... just ... wow."

The dress Eunice wore was old. It had been her formal attire on the first cruise she and her husband had ever taken. The 1974 Christian Dior Haute Couture evening gown had traveled with them on every cruise throughout the rest of his life. And now, it was at sea again. The chiffon gown was see-through with a satin sheath beneath. The neck and short sleeves were ruffled and a full pleated skirt draped from a satin bow at the waist. It was a deep green, a perfect reflection of days at sea ... and tonight the perfect background for the emerald, diamond and gold brooch nestled at its low-cut neck.

Eunice's only other adornment was her hair. Alita had managed to sleek the stubbly mane into a graceful sweep away from Eunice's face. Golden glitter, heavier around her hairline, now trailed off toward the back, like a comet with a bright tail. Alita beamed with pride. Eunice looked smashing. Lily could easily see the young beauty that the dress had graced all those decades ago. But that youngster could have never outclassed this goddess, standing so proud in front of her.

CHAPTER FIVE

✦ ✦ ✦

The Latin's Ranch gang met in the Star Power Lounge before dinner. All around them, fun seekers appeared relaxed, friendly and dressed to kill. Mementos from movies and rock stars decorated the room, and the plush furniture appeared to be stylized theatre seats and casting couches. Waiters, their red usher jackets sparkling with gold braid, hustled fru-fru drinks that looked benign but packed a serious punch. Rick wolf whistled at the women as they entered, and asked them each to dance to the live band.

Eunice accepted saying, "You must need the practice before dancing at your wedding."

Rick shushed her. "Don't want Alita to overhear. I haven't proposed just yet."

The two took the floor where Eunice could still execute a stylish waltz complete with underarm turns and pivots.

Next it was Lily's turn. "I'm not sure I can dance with this peg leg," she said, victimized by a sudden fear of falling.

"Your therapist told me you could," Rick said.

"Ernie told you that?"

"Yep. He said we're to cut a rug for him and send a picture to prove what a great physical therapist he is."

"Well, I can't let Ernie down," Lily said. She drew in a breath, rose from the red velvet chair and gave Rick her hand to enter the unknown of the dance floor.

It was delightful. Rick supported her with a strong measured lead in a basic box step, and she slowly melted from two stiff legs, one real and one artificial, into a smooth follow, then an unstructured sway of her body, then even a twirl. Fear gave way to the exhilaration of remembered motion. She heard the click and saw the flash near the end of the dance.

"Got it!" said Alita. "The photo is on its way to Ernie as we speak."

Bear was the last to arrive. When he made his entrance, Rick wolf whistled at him, too.

"Don't own a suit," Bear explained, ducking his head as if he were suddenly shy. "So I rented a tuxedo from the ship."

Lily thought he looked grand. The tailored black jacket suited his broad shoulders and minimized his girth. He stood a little taller, adding an inch to his already considerable height. Lily guessed he'd visited the spa for the excellent trim to his beard and hair.

And is that a manicure? Imagine!

The big man even managed one stately turn around the floor with each of the three ladies. In his arms, Alita drew the eyes of the crowd, dressed as she was in an airy cocktail dress whose ruffled hem extended no lower than mid-thigh. Afterwards, the rest sat in the comfortable lounge chairs, tickled to watch Rick and Alita take on the salsa numbers. Frankie, in a million dollar tux of his own, held the hand of his little dove and kept a protective eye on the stunning brooch she wore. Meanwhile, Vinny's eyes cut back and forth, watching every exit and entrance, no doubt isolating all the Hawk Noses aboard. Just before the dinner chimes, they ordered a second round of Shirley Temples, Bogarts and Rock of Ages. "I better stop before I'm three sheets to the wind," Lily whispered to Bear.

Aurora herself could not have out-cooked the Superstar chefs that evening if only because every entree was way outside the Latin's Ranch food budget. Alita had her first lobster, Lily and Eunice chose scampi, Rick tried Beef Wellington, and the rack of lamb went to Charlie. The rest ordered filet mignon. After dinner, they decided to meet in the Panorama Lounge at ten for a nightcap. In the meantime, they spread out across the ship enjoying the casino, piano bar or the "Hooray for Hollywood" song and dance revue in the theater. Charlie kept on the look-out for the woman he'd met at the Ketchikan dance hall.

Lily and Eunice minced back to their cabin to shed their dressy shoes and get the circulation in their feet going again. They changed to casual clothes, and Eunice deposited the albatross pin on the table next to its golden egg. Then they left to meet the others in the bar.

"Beautiful shoes come at a cost. Even sensible beautiful shoes," Lily observed, welcoming the feel of her old Clark loafers. This time when the two entered a lounge, it was not to dance but to relax. As they sank into easy chairs, Eunice said, "It's cool in here. Alita could you go to the cabin and get me a sweater or maybe my red shawl?"

"Sure, Miss Eunice." Alita jumped up and left on her errand happy as a young pointer on the hunt.

"I'd give you my jacket, Eunice, but I left it in the cabin," Bear said.

"I did too." Charlie said. "Where's your knight in shining armor to come to your rescue?"

"He was tired, poor darling. Retired for the evening," Eunice said.

Lily counted noses and noticed another one missing. "Vinny must be with him."

"Or out on deck yearning for his own little dove." Charlie winked at her.

Before the conversation turned to Vinny's romance with Sylvia, Lily changed its course. "Did you notice how the dealers responded to Frankie in the casino?"

"I noticed he was the only winner among us," Eunice said.

"And Charlie? Where's your dance hall girl?" Bear asked.

"Never saw her. The cruise is still young." He waggled his brows then yawned. "But I'm not. I'm beat. One drink and I'm out of here."

Eunice shivered. "Alita should be back. I wonder what's keeping her? It's only one deck down."

"I'll go help," Rick said. "Maybe she's bringing a selection. I know how much stuff you brought on board."

Eunice handed him her pass key as Charlie called, "Better call the front desk for a hand truck."

Lily stretched and stifled a yawn. She sighed and said, "This must be the best a cruise has to offer."

"Can't see how it could get much better," Bear agreed then sipped his Courvoisier.

✦ ✦ ✦

Rick zigzagged through the corridor which was as packed as an obstacle course. He avoided the laundry carts, room service trays, stewards preparing cabins for the night, and tipsy fun seekers seeking their cabins. One man, rushing out of a cabin and moving fast, forced Rick against the wall to make room to push by.

"Excuse me, asshat," Rick muttered, shaking his head.

Later Rick would blame himself. If he hadn't been drinking during the long evening, maybe he'd have reacted faster. Maybe he'd have noticed the man's hawk nose when they passed in the hall. Now, reaching the cabin the man had exited, Rick realized it was Eunice's room. He frowned, then stared down the hall at the fast moving man who was weaving through the same crowded hall that had slowed his own journey. Rick looked back to the cabin door and saw it was slightly open. He pushed it inward.

He saw her on the floor and froze. The material around her neck. The blood. Then his adrenalin spiked. A deep primal instinct told him to grieve later but catch the bastard who did this now. He pulled the door shut and took off flying down the hall.

As the man entered another cabin, Rick hit the door just before it closed. No other fuel worked like anger and pain. Rick had more than enough of both.

✦ ✦ ✦

The Latin's Ranch gang waited in the Panorama Lounge for Rick's return.

"Maybe we'll have to go find him as well as Alita," Eunice said.

"We better wait. First time they've been together alone in that room." Charlie wiggled his eye brows again and added, "Give them some time."

"Good thinking, Charlie."

"I wonder if tonight is proposal night," Lily said. "If so, I think Aurora will win the pool."

Their chat was interrupted by a call for Bear on the PA system.

"What the ...?" the big man said, pushing himself up. He waited as he steadied on his quad cane. When ready, he *kachunked* to the house phone in an alcove at the end of the bar.

"Bear Jacobs."

"I think she's dead. Help me."

"Rick?"

CHAPTER FIVE

"I killed him."

"Where are you?"

Rick stuttered a cabin number. Bear made a gesture toward Lily and she began to work her way from the chairs toward him. "I'm on my way, Rick. Touch nothing."

"There's blood ..."

"Stay there. We'll get through this."

Bear hung up and said to Lily who had arrived at his side, "Trouble. Keep Eunice here. Call Vinny to get up here and stand guard. Don't let her leave for the cabin."

"What is it?"

"Alita. Rick. It's bad."

"Then go," Lily said, paling as she turned to go back to Charlie and Eunice. As Bear left, he blessed her calm under fire. She'd ask questions later but not now, not when the stakes were high. He willed himself speed he could no longer muster for long.

I'm damn near useless anymore.

"Excuse me, excuse me, coming through," he blustered and a crowd of drinkers parted. The sea was rising so his lumbering amble was exaggerated by the sway of the ship.

"Just a fucking old drunk," he heard someone mutter as he pushed his way past.

He managed the staircase and corridor to arrive at the cabin gulping for air as he knocked. "Rick. It's me. Open up."

When the door cracked open, Bear nearly didn't recognize Rick. The features on the handsome young face were pulled into a tight, strained image of grief and fear. No more cocky, self-assured Rick. The retired PI pushed his way in, shut the door and scanned the room. He saw a desk chair on its side, curtain pulled from its rod, magazines and tour booklets strewn everywhere. A tipped vase had scattered a dozen roses across the floor and a champagne bottle lay amid them, open and empty.

Then Bear saw the body. He battled the heavy chair to turn it upright and said to Rick, "Sit."

The dead man was a marionette without the strings. Legs and arms were attached but connected to the torso at odd angles. Bones had been broken or at least wrenched from their sockets. A gash crossed the head, one that had bled profusely down his jacket. The body was half wedged between the bed and a wall, and although Bear tried to find a pulse at his neck, the guy was long past a working heart.

"Had a hawk nose," Bear said. "Broken now."

"He passed me in the hall. He'd just come out. Of Eunice's cabin. I looked and ..." A sob stopped the words in Rick's throat.

Bear grabbed his shoulders. "You did this?"

Rick nodded.

"Alita?"

"She's ... I think she's dead." Rick looked about to pass out. "She's dead, Bear. What will I -"

Bear shook him. "Breathe, goddamn it."

The aide did as he was told. One huge inhale. Exhale. Another.

"Okay. Give me the key to Eunice's room. Then stay here. Right here. Do nothing. Do you hear me? Rick?"

Rick nodded again. "She looked dead, Bear. What will I do? She's my life."

"Stay. Keep breathing deep and slow. Calm down. I'm gonna need you. I'll be back as soon as I can."

Bear had no choice but to leave the boy alone while he made his way to Eunice's cabin. He unlocked the door and entered the suite.

It smelled of perfumes and powders as though three women had dressed for a gala evening just hours ago. But the merriment had ended. Bear's tears nearly blinded him as he looked down on the fallen girl at his feet. He thought of a little bird, its neck broken from dashing against glass. Bear sat on the sofa, body aching from exertion. Leaning down, he gently touched Alita's silky hair, then reached to pull down the hem of her dress. He wished he could give her the dignity that murder victims were never allowed, as investigative specialists victimized them yet again. Bear wanted to cradle the broken youngster whose song was silent forever.

The big man shook his head to clear his thoughts. He took his own advice and breathed a great breath. Time to get to work. Trickles of blood had dried at Alita's nose and ears, sure signs of strangulation. A filmy scarf was still around her, cruelly collapsing the windpipe. Or was it a nylon? If so, the guy didn't come prepared for murder. He found his weapon in the room where he hadn't expected to find a woman. At least not this woman.

That's what the Boston Strangler used, wasn't it? A nylon. And tied it in a bow. Stop it. Focus.

A deep gash in Alita's hand had bled abundantly, soaking into her dress. The wound was the twin of the one on the dead man's cheek. Bear noticed blood under her nails as he checked her wrist for the pulse he knew was no longer there. "You fought back didn't you, brave girl? You got him with whatever you held."

A noise in the hall. Bear lurched for the door as it cracked opened. Lily blocked someone's view into the room as she said, "No, Alejandro. We don't need room service this evening, we're just too tired. See you in the morning." She put the Do Not Disturb sign out, slithered through the door and shut it quickly.

Bear reached her to say she shouldn't have come. She started to tell him Charlie was with Eunice but then she saw Alita. After that, all he could do was hold her. Somewhere in his copious brain he realized they held each other, and each was trembling.

"Oh Bear! Not this. She can't be ..." Lily whispered. "Such a lovely child."

"She is, Lily. She's dead. And we need to be clear headed. Right now. For her. For Rick."

He felt her spine stiffen with resolve. "Tell me what to do."

"Go back and round up the group. Have everyone come to my suite. Charlie has a key. All of you wait for me there. Tell them as much as you know. But keep everyone away from this cabin."

"Where are you going?"

"Back to Rick."

"He didn't ... he didn't ..."

"Do this? Of course not. But he killed the man who did."

"No! Then he needs you. Go."

They left the cabin together. Before they parted in the hall, Bear said, "Lily? Send Vinny to meet me." He gave her the cabin number for the hawk nosed man, then he returned to it himself.

When Bear entered the cabin, Rick was right where he'd left him, elbows on his knees and hands covering his face. But the body was gone. And the sliding door to the balcony was open.

"Rick, what the fuck happened? What have you done?"

"It was wrong for me to get you involved, Bear. You're not to blame for any of this. So I dumped the body. Overboard. I killed him for Alita. Sharks can have the piece of shit now."

Bear opened and closed his mouth like a dying trout before sound finally made its way out. Then it was a growl. "Don't you know they have cameras aimed damn near everywhere on a ship?"

Rick looked up, pleading for understanding. "Fuck, Bear. My life is over. I don't care. Besides, it's after midnight. Nobody will ever look at those tapes."

"Oh yeah, smart guy? What about when they come up one passenger short?"

"Then they won't -"

"Shut it. We'll talk about it later. Right now we have things to do if we're gonna save your sorry ass."

Anger seemed to shove anguish aside. Rick snarled. "The bastard deserved to die."

"I agree. But that's beside the point. Alita didn't deserve to die, but she *does* deserve you to be safe. Everyone knows how she loved you. Here's what we're going to do."

✦ ✦ ✦

They wiped down anything Rick might have touched in Hawk Nose's room. Vinny joined them, and he was far more expert in how to hide a murder than Bear would ever be. "They may suspect, but they will not know. For now," the Italian said, judging the room to be tidied enough to leave it behind.

All three went to Bear's suite where Lily had succeeded in gathering the other Latin's Ranch residents together. A shockwave of their grief, confusion and fury hit him as he entered his cabin.

CHAPTER FIVE

"Is it true Bear? Is Alita dead on this god forsaken boat?" Eunice gasped, tears following channels through the wrinkles on her cheeks. "Is it true?" Lily came forward to gather Rick in a motherly hug although he towered over her. "Oh, dear boy. Poor boy."

Frankie gestured to Vinny. "You find this man, you feed him to the fishes."

"Rick has already seen to that. Everyone sit down. We need to talk." Bear took command of the room, and even Frankie allowed it to happen. The old capo might know about committing crimes, but Bear knew about solving them.

Bear brought them all up to speed as best he could.

"Why Bear? Why did this happen?" Lily asked.

He shrugged. "Could be this." From his pocket he pulled a handkerchief and unwrapped it to reveal the albatross brooch. "Rick found it in the man's pocket before pitching the body overboard." He handed it to Frankie, hoping Eunice wouldn't see the blood crusted on the sharp tips of the gold and jeweled wings.

Frankie looked up at Bear, appalled. "You mean he came to the cabin to steal this from my little dove?"

"Maybe. He stole it, yes. But maybe it wasn't what he truly was after." Bear chose not to share any more of his suspicions at the moment. "But I'll find out."

Frankie said, "You are good detective, Bear, I think. You will find this answer. Vinny will be your, how you say, posse, yes?"

"Tell them what you know about the brooch, Rick. It's important."

Rick was a portrait of desolation. He looked caved in as though a team of mules had kicked him in the solar plexus. In a voice made raspy from crying, he said, "When you gave Eunice the pin, Signore Tononi, she passed it around for us all to see. I recognized it. I mean I'd been told about it years ago when I was a little kid. Part of our Alutiiq mythology. The fur trader you mentioned, the one who brought it to Alaska? The woman he married was a tribal princess, a grandmother of my grandmothers. After the marriage, he was shunned by the other Russians. You were told his wife died of disease and that the brooch disappeared after her death. But Alutiiqs know she died trying to keep the bird from thieves. If it had stayed with my family, it would have been honored always, never sold as a trinket."

As Rick crumpled onto an ottoman in front of Lily, Bear said to the group, "Maybe Hawk Nose was a thief, too. Knew the value of such an heirloom when he saw it tonight on Eunice. Waited 'til we were up in the Panorama Lounge and broke into this cabin to steal it. But Alita was here, in the way. I think she had it in her hand, probably putting it away when he barged in. He has a slice to his head and she has a gash across her hand. I think she tried to hold on to it, used it as a weapon against him." His voice caught. "She was a resourceful girl. No push over."

"We need to call ship security," Charlie said. He reached out for the phone.

"Just a minute, Charlie," Lily said putting a hand on top of his. "I think we need to talk about Rick."

"What about him?"

"You're right, Lily," Bear said. "Rick murdered the man who murdered Alita. Took matters in his own hands. Illegal, of course. But do we each think this homicide was justified?" He waited while they looked back and forth, a jury deliberating its verdict. Then he added, pushing his viewpoint just a little more. "Do we want him to go to prison maybe forever? The tribes don't always do well under white laws."

There was a time when Bear would have never considered hiding a homicide. It was the law. As a licensed investigator who worked with both attorneys and law enforcers, he was bound to support it. But he was much older now, had too often seen right go terribly wrong. For Bear, the law of the land was not as powerful as the law of nature. Rick would likely be hunted until he paid the price. But the hunter would not be Bear.

Eunice, Frankie, Lily and Charlie reached a conclusion. "Hell no," they said, almost in unison. "Bastard deserved it," Eunice added.

"But our silence could make us accessories after the fact. We'll all have to play dumb."

"Especially easy in my case," Charlie said, under no illusions about his brain power.

"Maybe we'll be keel hauled after all," Lily said. "No matter. Tell us how we protect our boy."

"Okay, then. If we're agreed. Nobody can know about Alita until after we dock in Juneau ... " He looked at his watch. "Six hours from now. We

CHAPTER FIVE

need to get Rick off this ship before Alita is found and security closes the ship down. So Eunice and Lily, you need to go to your room now, walk right past the body, don't look at it or touch anything. Go into your bedroom and go to bed."

Eunice gasped.

Bear continued. "I know it won't be easy, but you must. When you 'wake up' at nine, you'll find the body in your living room and report it. She came in during the night. You don't know when. Never heard a thing." The two women nodded as they received their orders.

"Vinny, Rick and I will get off the ship at eight with the other passengers. Security won't be alerted to anything yet. None of you know or saw anything. That includes you, Charlie. And you, Frankie. Security will get to you eventually. Is that clear?"

"We know nothing about the nothing we see," Frankie confirmed.

"Lily, they'll ask lots of questions. Be sure neither of you draw undue attention to Rick while telling them about Alita. But don't disavow him altogether if his name comes up. They know we're traveling together."

"Of course, Bear. We'll do our best," Lily said. "After we report the death, I'll get on the phone to Latin's Ranch. I'll try to get Chrissie up here. We'll need an aide to replace, well, you know."

"Good. Smart," Bear nodded. "And another thing. You all must continue your day as planned. Catch your ride and go sightseeing. Eunice, pick up your award. We have to act as normal as we can. Sad, yes, over the loss of an aide. But no more emotionally involved than that."

Frankie looked down at the brooch in his hand then over to Eunice. She shrugged and smiled wistfully at him. The old man stood, body vibrating with the effort, crossed to Rick and handed the brooch to the boy. "Here. Take this. Ez yours. I, too, understand family honor."

CHAPTER SIX

Case Notes
May 14, 3 a.m.

Our cabin is a suite. Eunice and I share a large bedroom with a separate living room. That's where Alita sleeps. Slept. Now she's dead out there on the floor. We had to come in here and ignore her. Try to sleep. How could we possibly? Even before this, the floor was rocky, what with being a ship and all. We already felt off balance. Now a loved one has fallen with no warning. It all feels like a Fun House with tilting walls and threatening passageways. I never dreamed I'd suffer from such powerlessness again. But the Grim Jokester is always just around the corner.
Alita was with us since the nursing home. She moved to Latin's Ranch and became an indispensible part of the crew. Her youth and joy soothed us when the crushing realities of old age overtook us. It feels like the fragile bubble of our happy home has burst. We are diminished, as though the air has been let out of our bodies.
Eunice is, I think, especially aggrieved. This cruise was her idea and she is feeling the weight of that guilt. I'm not sure anyone can help her with that, but I'll try.
Without an aide, neither of us was able to prepare for night all that well. Simple washing and toileting became a major effort. But we did it. Hung up our dress clothes, too, which were in a pile on the beds.
"What will happen to Rick in Juneau?" Eunice said to me in a low

CHAPTER SIX

voice thick with emotion.
My own voice was low as well. There was no real need to whisper but it seemed the right thing to do so late on such a distressing night. "Well, there's no way out of town but by boat or air. There are no roads." It was imperative he get away fast. After either murder was known to the authorities, he'd definitely be a person of interest. "Bear will figure it out."
Since we couldn't sleep, we worried through the empty hours. I updated these case notes and Eunice added the wooden beads to Baby Benny's sweater. It was adorable. The baby will never know the tears that were shed as the final needlework was done.

- Lily Gilbert, Brokenhearted Assistant to PI Bear Jacobs

Charlie and Bear went back to their own suite with Rick. The aide mustered enough strength to help Charlie get to bed, then he joined Bear in the living room. He collapsed on the sofa, nearly overpowering it with his size. Bear knew no one but Charlie would sleep much, but he wanted to see Rick settled in, so he called room service and told them to hustle up a bucket of beers. Maybe two buckets.

He listened to Rick's ramblings, a silent audience as the young man mourned. Rick talked about the days between the nursing home and Latin's Ranch, when he and Alita had explored the campgrounds and beaches of the Pacific coastline. How she never quite got a dresser drawer or kitchen cabinet door shut. How she loved old *Cheers* episodes on TV and making apple pies with lattice crusts and wearing his raggedy Peninsula College t-shirt and hearing his Alutiiq myths of the Raven and the Thirsty Whale.

Through a haze, bleary with beer and tears, Rick looked at Bear. "She adored you old fossils, Bear. Called you her grams and gramps. Said she'd never known how wise and kind old people were. You treated her like she mattered."

"Because she did," Bear said when he could control his voice.

In time, Rick drifted off. Bear kept watch from the easy chair near the sofa.

Rick was not a boy. He was a grown man. He had to own what he had done and handle what he had lost. In the morning, he needed to disappear for good. Bear could just say farewell at the dock, but he thought he'd stick a bit longer. He'd get Rick to a seaplane. Buy him a ticket to Kodiak. Tell him to disappear into the land of his ancestors. If and when he was found, he'd be on their reservation. Maybe more could be done for him with tribal lawyers and independent nation status.

Rick might not make it. Bear knew that. But this was an action plan and the tired old man felt hopeful as he drifted off to sleep. Anything that could give him a little hope right this moment was worth its weight in Alaskan gold.

✦ ✦ ✦

Lily and Eunice watched the dawn through the glass door of their bedroom balcony. Narrow channels of glacial water cut through icy, rugged mountains. The beauty of the place offered them some solace, as though their eyes could help heal their hearts.

By nine, their resolve stiffened, the two old friends were ready for their day to begin. Holding tight to each other, they went out to their living room. The balcony curtain was open and light poured in. The ship was now docked at the Juneau harbor where a stern rock wall overhung the little community's perch on the edge of Gastineau Channel. Tourists were disembarking for a fun day of excursions.

Together the women turned from the view to look at Alita, still there on the floor. Her body had gone through the death chill by now, bringing it to room temperature. Blood, without circulation to keep it going, had pooled and settled where her injured hand touched the floor. Her facial muscles had lost all tension so she looked smooth, impossibly young. In silence Eunice and Lily said good-bye. Then Lily called for ship security.

Eunice sat on the sofa as Lily went to the cabin door to remove the Do Not Disturb sign. Their steward Alejandro was just outside next to his room cart filled with fresh towels, new mini-shampoos, body lotions, con-

CHAPTER SIX

ditioners. Cylindrical vases of fresh flowers stood in soldier-straight rows on the cart's top shelf, ready to be dispensed suite to suite.

"Good morning, Miss Lily," the Filipino said with a joyful lilt. "Did you have a wonderful evening? We are in Juneau on a sunny day. Unheard of! You are going ashore today?" As he chattered, the blissful expression on his handsome brown face slowly melted into a frown. "But what is wrong, my lady? You do not look well."

Lily opened the door all the way and held it, motioning him in. He looked to Eunice. "And Miss Eunice, you too look so ... AAEEE!" When he saw Alita, he made a dash toward her.

"Stop!" cried Lily. "You shouldn't touch anything, Alejandro. The authorities wouldn't like that."

"That's correct, ma'am. You must have had dealings with law enforcement before."

Lily jumped as the security team appeared at the open cabin door. A man and a woman, each in a blindingly white shirt, unflattering black pants, laden with radios and mysterious devices on their tool belts. They had set their faces in stern expressions as though it was Rule One in the Ship Security Handbook: authority figures should appear unpleasant. Lily knew she was in trouble just from the looks of them.

"In fact, steward, leave. Now. Before you feel the need to clean anything." The male officer actually made shooing gestures with his hands, doing away with Alejandro.

It irritated Lily. "Gosh. The caste system must still be in effect on cruise ships."

That irritated Mr. Security. "I'm going to ask you two ladies to vacate the immediate area, as well. Please go to the bedroom."

Ms. Security was no better. "Please. Stay quiet and out of the way while we take a look."

The ladies did as told, each sitting on the foot of her bed. "You've never been good with authority figures," Eunice whispered.

"Doesn't look like that's going to change."

"Play dumb, be dumb," Eunice reminded her.

"I can know nothing without being nice about it."

For the first time since last night, Eunice smiled. And it was at Lily. Lily returned the favor and a little of the starch returned to their spines. It was the magic of friendship.

Ms. Security appeared in the doorway. "Have you touched anything out there?"

"Of course. This is our suite," Lily said. "I'd say we've touched almost everything."

"I mean the body, ma'am. Did you touch the body?"

"It's not the body. She's Alita Aarons. Our aide and friend." Eunice's lip crumpled. "And no, we didn't touch her."

"Do you know who did this?"

"Of course not. Nobody we know would hurt Alita."

"Well then, looks like somebody you didn't know did it," said Mr. Security, swaggering into the bedroom, belly jiggling over his tool belt. "Now we're really getting somewhere."

"How wonderful to have skilled investigators on board."

Ms. Security ignored or didn't hear the acid in Lily's comment. She turned to her partner. "Better alert the captain. And Juneau. They can decide whether to involve those FBI buttinskies."

"You ladies wait here," Mr. Security ordered.

"Maybe I best wait here, too." Ms. Security cut her eyes suspiciously toward Eunice then Lily as though the two oldsters might make a break for it. "Don't plan on leaving your cabin anytime soon, ladies."

That surprised them. "But ... but I have an award ceremony to attend today," Eunice piped up.

"Award, ma'am?"

"Yes, the Arctic Angel Award. From PASTA."

"You getting an award for your pasta?"

"No, no, no. From the Protective Association of the Short-Tailed Albatross."

The two officers looked at each other then back to Eunice. "Well ma'am one of them albatrosses may have to fly it over here to you," said Ms. Security.

"Cause you aren't getting off this ship today," said Mr. Security.

CHAPTER SIX

✦ ✦ ✦

Baby Benny enjoyed nothing more than one of his own farts.

"Boo goo boo," he chortled.

"OMG," gasped Chrissie. "Maybe no more of the pureed sweet potatoes." The aide handed the baby back to his mother.

Jessica chortled, too, tucking Benny in one arm while fanning the air with the other. "Guess I'll add air fresheners to the Costco list."

The day after the residents sailed away, Jessica zeroed in on the serious housekeeping she could accomplish without distractions. She and Chrissie walked through the house together, listing projects to tackle while it was as vacant as it ever got.

"I'll organize work teams for the deep cleaning and painting," Jessica said before scuttling away to attend Benny's smelly needs. "We'll start tomorrow."

The next day, Work Team Number One turned out to be just Aurora. The cook told Jessica that her kitchen was already deep cleaned, thank you very much, and that if there was any more to do, she would do it herself. She emptied the store rooms, pantry, cabinets, freezers and refrigerators each in its own turn. No surface was left unscrubbed, unsanitized, unbuffed, or unsparkled.

For Work Team Number Two, Jessica recruited Chrissie's boyfriend, Will Haverstock. Together, he and Chrissie would spiff up the common areas by painting the living and dining room walls.

The two had met about a year ago at Reggie's Tavern, and their attraction had been instantaneous. Bear, who had been there to see the event, had observed, "It was a case of strange calling to strange."

Like magnets, Chrissie and Will had stuck ever since. They'd both suffered miserable paths to arrive at this blissful union of trust and love. Chrissie was tall but she slouched, looking so self conscious she might cave in. As a child, Will had been beaten so badly by his father that he had a permanent limp and an unnatural bend to his nose. Chrissie had been dumped with two youngsters to raise; Will cared for the grandparents who'd raised him after his parents left him behind. Chrissie was a caregiver to the living; Will was an embalmer to the dead. Since they'd found each other, the one stood a little taller and the other walked a little straighter.

"They both respect old people," Jessica had said to Ben. "The difference is that Chrissie's are alive."

Will worked for a funeral home but only part time. More and more people were choosing cremations which didn't require embalmers. He worried that there would not be enough work to keep him employed at all. In the meantime, he hustled for other jobs to shore up his shaky income. Painting the walls at a senior home suited him just fine, especially at Latin's Ranch where he knew and liked the owners and residents. And especially when he could work alongside his honey.

This morning, Chrissie and Will were ready to begin. "We gonna paint it blue and red again?" Will asked, craning his neck here and there to observe the walls. He was so slender his Adam's apple appeared to dance. Jessica had trouble not watching it.

"It was never blue and red. It's turquoise and coral," Chrissie corrected Will.

"More specifically, Desert Gemstone and Chili Pepper," Jessica corrected Chrissie. She was jigging Baby Benny up and down on her hip, holding him with one hand and paint samples in the other.

"So, Desert Gemstone and Chili Pepper?" Will asked. "And please notice, I'm not rolling my eyes."

"No, I think this time maybe Biscayne Shore and Hot Spice." Jessica handed Will the paint fan deck, spread out to the two samples. "You two go buy the paint and supplies. Ben and I will de-moss and stain the porch."

As Jessica left the room, she overheard Will whisper, "Does she realize these are the same colors?"

"Don't tell her. She's happy," Chrissie said. "Let's go."

Jessica's decorating confidence faltered as she watched Will's bilious green clown car bounce down the drive. At least she didn't take color advice from him. But maybe she should have consulted with Sylvia, the decorator who had helped in the first place. Then again, no. Sometimes change was not a good thing. The rooms looked bright and happy to her. And wasn't that the way a care facility should look? More lively than subdued,

CHAPTER SIX

more promising than serene?

Having justified her decision, she went in search of Ben, hoping he'd be willing to de-moss the deck now. She was optimistic that he'd like the new Butternut stain. Crossing through the hall, baby in tow, she heard her office phone ring. She detoured to pick it up. "Latin's Ranch," she said.

"Gaburble goo," said Baby Benny.

"Jess, it's Lily."

"Lily! How are you? Benny says hi, too."

"We need help. Can Chrissie fly to Juneau? She has to get here before the ship leaves tomorrow."

"Fiff, fiff, plerg," said Baby Benny before he let out a mighty shriek.

Jessica felt like a mighty shriek herself as she listened to Lily explain that Alita had died.

✦ ✦ ✦

Late in the morning, Lily and Eunice were released from their cabin. In fact, they were evicted.

"It's a crime scene, you know," said Ms. Security. "You need to go so authorities can investigate."

"I'm pleased to know that you recognize it as such," Lily sniped. "When will the real authorities arrive?"

Ms. Security replied, "The local law is already on board. They'll be here when they're finished at the buffet."

"But where shall we go? What shall we do?" Eunice, a great one for drama, managed a little sob as she raised a graceful hand to her puckered forehead. Lily hoped she didn't take it too far, but Ms. Security seemed oblivious that two little old ladies were capable of insolence.

"This ship is full of food and activities even on port days. Go for it. Just don't head ashore. We'd catch you before you disembarked the ship. We need to know where you are. There'll be questions."

Lily and Eunice left the cabin, running straight into Alejandro who was hovering just outside their door. He clucked and fretted about poor Miss

Alita as the three of them headed down the hall. It was empty now, but Lily could imagine it full of obstacles as Rick chased Hawk Nose through it last night.

Ah, Rick. Good-bye, my boy. Be safe.

The three took the elevator up to the Superstar Diner, the ship's aft buffet where food was available nearly day and night. Alejandro seemed bound and determined to mother hen his ladies; it was his job and he did it well.

"Have you heard anything more, Alejandro? Has anyone else been ... ah ... hurt?" Lily asked as they zipped to the top of the ship. The glass door allowed them to see the front desk and main lobby far below.

"You expect more foul play?" Alejandro's eyes opened so wide the whites gleamed all the way around. "Oh, no, Miss Lily. Please do not worry. One murder maybe. But two are far below Celestial standards."

The elevator doors opened on Deck 11, right at the entrance of the enormous buffet area. A tiny Indonesian girl scurried to them like they were long lost friends and slathered their hands with Purell. Her smile let her get away with it before every meal even though it irked many passengers who saw no reason for such nonsense. Lily figured that if the girl could manage sanitizing this crowd without incident, then Celestial should promote her to head of Guest Relations by season's end.

The Superstar Diner was decorated like an old time drug store fountain area, in case a Hollywood producer happened along to discover the next starlet. White tile counters, marble table tops and chrome trim made the area bright and airy. Dinette chairs had cherry red padded seats like diner stools, but were far larger and, as Lily already knew from a battle earlier in the cruise, they were heavy enough to resist lumpy seas.

Frankie and Charlie were already at a table and waved them over. Alejandro pulled chairs out for them then galloped away to get them a late breakfast.

"Well, at least Hawk Nose hasn't been missed yet," Lily said as she sat. "Otherwise Alejandro would know about it."

"When I woke up, Rick helped me get ready. Then he left with Bear." Charlie was eating prunes on oatmeal. "Gonna miss that young man."

"They come by for Vinny. They are gone long by now," said Frankie. "Off the ship and away. Ez for the best." He reached across the table to pat

CHAPTER SIX

Eunice's hand. "Good morning, my little dove."

"Perfect," Lily said. "Now we just go about our day. Except Eunice and I can't leave the ship."

"Oh, that's right!" Eunice pulled a cell phone in a zebra-striped case out of her craft bag. "I must call Dr. Flavenmire."

"You need a doctor?" Frankie's eyebrows tented in worry like an upside down W.

"No, my dear. Dr. Leland Flavenmire is the director of the Protective Association of the Short-Tailed Albatross. I must tell him I won't be there to accept my award. This is all my fault."

Lily knew that none of the Latin's Ranch gang could ever stand to see Eunice sad. She was so often the sparkplug of their little group, keeping them up when ailments and circumstances got them down. Charlie said, "Don't worry, Eunice. Maybe he can reschedule for tomorrow."

"That's right," Lily added, wanting to kiss Charlie's old cheek for thinking of that. "The ship spends the night here. Doesn't leave until late afternoon. Maybe Dr. Flavenmire could change the award day."

Charlie added, "I'm hoping to paint the town tonight with the gal I met in Ketchikan. If I ever find her again."

"Good idea, Charlie. I'll go over there to place a call so you guys can keep talking." Eunice indicated an alcove near the huge windows where a stack of high chairs was stored.

Lily gave passing thought to how many high chairs were actually necessary for a ship whose passengers averaged the age of sixty. Then she said to Frankie and Charlie, "Our driver in Ketchikan planned for a car to meet us here in Juneau at eleven. But now, Eunice and I can't go. I think you two should take the car and enjoy a private excursion." She zeroed in on Charlie. "Act natural. Don't talk about Rick in front of the driver or anyone."

"I do not want to leave my little dove unprotected." Frankie's face puckered as much as one of Charlie's prunes.

"Frankie, we'll be fine. The danger is off the ship. Hawk Nose is somewhere at the bottom of the ocean. Besides, Vinny and Bear will be back soon." She stopped long enough to shrug. "And, well, we don't look so fragile if we're not all together. We can't let someone start to wonder where our other aide is. So you two should go."

"She's right, Frankie," Charlie said. He leaned over and said man to man, "Besides, I understand they got saloons here."

Eunice returned. "Well, he isn't happy. But Dr. Flavenmire understands the situation. He said he will try to reschedule the ceremony for tomorrow." She sat with a sigh. "Is it wrong of me to really want to go get this award? After all that's happened because of me?"

"Of course not, Eunice. Life goes on. Nobody knows better than we do. Nothing is your fault."

"I feel so dreadful about everything."

"The cruise was a brilliant idea, Eunice. It has given us all lots to do and see ... more than we ever thought we'd do again."

"Nobody's blaming you for a murder, then another, then the disappearance of Rick," Charlie pitched in.

Lily sighed. Charlie could go just so far before going bad. "Very comforting, Charlie."

"I aim to please."

CHAPTER SEVEN

Case Notes
May 14, 4 p.m.

Frankie and Charlie left the Superstar Diner to get ready for their excursion. I told them the driver's name is Dimitri. "He'll be wearing a yellow sweater and holding a sign with Eunice's name. I'll call him to say you two are taking the tour today instead of us."
When they were gone, I made the call, then Eunice and I consulted the Celestial Stargazer daily program of activities.
"I'd rather sit here and pout," Eunice pouted.
I know what she meant. I'm sad for Alita and angry for Rick. And I'm worried about saying the wrong thing to the authorities and blowing the whole damn deal. But Bear told us to act natural. So I reminded her, "We need to appear like we're enjoying our cruise. We have to circulate."
Eunice loved nothing as much as drama. She squared her shoulders, touched her cheek with the back of a hand and said, "I'm ready for my close-up, Lily." Then she studied the activities with me.
I said, "Let's take this craft class on making ocean-theme key rings from pasta shells."
"Sure. I could teach a class like that myself."
After the craft class, we went to the culinary theatre to learn how to make sushi. "An oft needed skill at Latin's Ranch," I said to Eunice. But I have to admit, the activity made me feel better than sitting

around brooding.

We were learning how to fold towels into animals when security hunted us down. "The Juneau deputies are waiting for you in your cabin," Ms. Security said. "I suggest you hurry. Before we have to feed them lunch, too."

"We'll be there when we get there," I replied. I mean really. We couldn't leave until we knew exactly how to create the elephant's trunk, now could we?

- Lily Gilbert, Crafty Assistant to PI Bear Jacobs

The wide, welcoming dock area at Juneau was overrun by a tsunami of passengers when the cruise ship opened its doors for disembarkation. The masses split into two groups heading in different directions, as surely as political parties.

"This group is gonna strip the town bare of wolf t-shirts and hand carved otters," Bear groused, using his quad cane as a barrier between his body and hundreds of souvenir junkies galloping toward shops. Then, along with Vinny and Rick, he cut through the group of sightseers who wore numbered tags stuck to their slickers and hoodies. The tags matched up to the numbers on their excursion buses. Cruise personnel were herding them into queues; they were battling back to get the best seats.

The three men employed the broken field running techniques they'd learned from years of watching the NFL. Getting to the curb unscathed, they looked for a cab. There was a queue for them, too.

"We need to get Rick out of here," Bear murmured to either Vinny or himself. "Before --"

"Pssst. Need a ride gents?" An old sourdough asked them.

Bear looked him up and down. In the spirit of the town, the driver was dressed like a gold prospector, complete with red long johns, leather vest, floppy hat and wild grey beard. "You a prospector or a cabbie?"

"Either way, it's panning for gold. Unofficial like. If you need a ride, follow me away from the crowd."

He walked them to an alley where an ancient Windstar minivan slumped on its weary wheels. On the way he chattered. "Welcome to Juneau, gents, home of the twenty minute summer, ha ha! See you like braces, too!" he said to Bear, apparently delighted by the big man's suspenders as he snapped his own.

"Yeah. But mine aren't red and don't have kicking jackasses on them," Bear replied.

"Why, we can stop and get you some at Dead Eye Dolly's Emporium of Peculiars. Climb aboard Jenny now for the tour of a lifetime."

Everyone loaded into the sagging van. Vinny and Rick took the back seat while Bear maneuvered himself into the front. The driver said, "You boys just call me Driver Dan, and we'll be on our way. Glad you jumped ship early. Best time for wildlife viewing. Early bird gets the moose, ha ha!"

"Good one," Rick muttered. It was the first thing he'd said since leaving the ship.

"Now where do we begin? Mendenhall Glacier? Gold Creek? Governor's Mansion? Tram to -"

"We need to catch a flight," Bear interrupted.

"Gonna vamoose, huh? Cruisin' not your cup of hooch, huh? Did you leave your valises on the dock?"

"No luggage." Bear had not let Rick leave with more than a Celestial tote bag in order to avoid unwanted questions as they left the ship.

"Got it. Undercover, like. Airport's just eight miles away. Giddyup, Jenny." The old van shuddered, coughed, and lurched into traffic. "What airline ... like we have lots of different terminals, ha ha!"

"Not an airline. Sea plane, more likely."

"Plenty of those out there, too. Got a runway that's a pond, believe it or not."

"A private charter."

"Our largest charter service -"

"Smallest, I'm thinking. Maybe just a guy with a plane. And not a lot of questions."

Driver Dan dropped the prospector routine. "Right. I get the picture. No Tell Air. Say no more."

The drive took them out of town, hairpinned over a mountain, slid down the other side to an inlet off the main channel. Bear was aware of the gorgeous views but was so worried he didn't really take in the sights.

Would the van internally hemorrhage? Would Rick make it to Kodiak? Was Lily keeping Charlie, Frankie and Eunice together? Was Eunice still in danger? Was Baby Benny doing okay back home without him?

Take a cruise. Relax. Bullshit.

When Driver Dan eased Jenny to a stop, it was next to a rickety shed built from deadwood, corrugated metal and spit. A short dock led to a DeHavilland Beaver.

"Where is this?" Bear asked, looking at the shack.

"What is that?" Rick asked, looking at the seaplane.

"Who is that?" Vinny asked, squinting at the scraggly teenager heading their way.

"This here is cousin Luke's place. That there is his plane. A 1959 DeHavilland, best damn bush plane ever built. And that's Luke coming this way."

"Ez very young boy to fly very old plane," Vinny muttered. Bear rarely heard him sound concerned for anyone but Frankie.

"Young?" Rick said, sounding pretty damn concerned as well. "He's a child! A fifth grader."

"Don't you worry about young Luke, boyo. He'll fly you through the eye of a needle if you want. Ask you no questions as long as you don't ask him for a current license. Or expect him to serve peanuts during the flight."

There was a degree less mayhem but still plenty of activity when Driver Dan dropped Bear and Vinny back at the cruise ship. The dock area was broad and inviting with pedestrians and vehicles going this way and that. Horse drawn buggies clopped along, rental scooters and segues laced in and out, even a Humvee muscled its way through the area. Cabs grabbed up passengers and whisked them away like eagles swooping down on fish.

Bear was glad of so much activity because he needed the distraction. He'd been mourning over Rick ever since Vinny and he stood on the rickety little pier and watched the DeHavilland roar away, floundering through the water with the grace of an overweight goose taking flight.

CHAPTER SEVEN

Rick was scared. Bear knew that. Probably more scared of leaving everything he knew than of the old rattletrap seaplane. He'd make it to Kodiak, Bear was pretty sure. He was also pretty sure the envelope Vinny had handed Rick was cash from Frankie. But what would life be like for the young man from now on? Some stories had no ending and for an old investigator like Bear, not knowing was almost intolerable.

Bear might have missed them as he trudged back to the ship, but Vinny saw them waving. "Look, Signore Bear. Ez my padrone. With Signore Charlie."

Sure enough, Charlie was waving his arms and yelling, "Hey! Hey Bear! BEAR!" Around him cruisers leaped away, terrified by the sighting of a bear on the Juneau dock. They bounded off, providing a circle of calm around Charlie, Frankie and the tour guide in bright yellow, holding a sign that said EUNICE TAYLOR in magic marker. Charlie was in his wheelchair and Frankie leaned heavily on a sturdy walker, one with a seat if he needed it.

Vinny dashed forward to offer support to his boss. Bear caught up, *kachunking* along on his cane. Truth be known, he was feeling damn tired after a night with so little sleep.

"Come with us, guys," Charlie said. "The girls can't leave the ship so we have their ride. This guy is Dimitri. He's gonna show us around. Then we can look for wildlife ... you know, chicks in a saloon."

The driver said, "You're welcome to join, but I'll have to charge more for four of you. Company policy."

"There will not be four. Vinny, you will go to my little dove. Be sure she ez safe. But, Bear, you may accompany us if you so choose."

Go or stay?

With Vinny onboard, Bear was not worried about Eunice's welfare. And the further Bear stayed away from the investigating authorities, the less likely he'd get pissed off. Or piss them off. A ride with Charlie and Frankie seemed like a better idea.

"Can't let you guys paint the town without me," Bear said.

The three men slowly worked their way to the Toyota Highlander, while Dimitri loaded the wheelchair and walker into the back. Bear kept his cane in the front seat with him.

This drive through town was far more relaxing than the earlier one that morning with Driver Dan. Bear found himself enjoying it as he considered how unique a place Juneau was. A state capitol with no dome, a huge governor's mansion that could hold about half the Alaskan population, no highway through the mountain rock and glacial ice to connect it to the rest of the state.

Dimitri pulled the car atop a high rock outcropping for a panoramic view. Bear was grateful that the driver was sensitive to the handicaps of his three passengers. He parked close enough to the rock retaining wall so the three could look from the car without struggling out and back in.

"There's our ship," Charlie exclaimed as they viewed the little town and the enormous cruise ship dwarfing it.

"See three or four of them from here some days in the summer," Dimitri was saying when a tremendous bang sent the car jerking forward into the retaining wall.

"What the..." one of them said and the SUV banged forward again.

Bear looked back to see the grill of an enormous vehicle punching into the backend of the Highlander. "It's the Humvee! From the ship dock." He saw its driver leap out, rifle in hand. "Get out. Run!" Bear yelled, knowing only Dimitri was spry enough to try it.

Dimitri never moved.

The driver from the Humvee pulled open Bear's door, and growled, "Get out." A ski mask covered the facial features.

"Can't do it, my friend. Too hobbled up."

"You're a fucking guy," Ski Mask said in what sounded like surprise. "And you in the back ... you're men!"

"Yeah, asshole. Dangerous men," squeaked Charlie in a voice half an octave higher than usual.

"Goddamn it to hell." Ski Mask said, spitting out the words like shrapnel before slamming Bear's door closed and turning away.

That's when they noticed at least half a dozen tourists taking photos. Ski Mask took off for the Humvee and roared away.

There was a moment of silence before Bear said, "First time I've been glad to see a cell phone in every pair of hands. Charlie, you okay back there?"

CHAPTER SEVEN

"Considering the backend of the car is here in the backseat with us, I'm fine. Our mobility equipment is toast though."

"Frankie, what about you?"

"The next time I go for drive, it ez with Vinny. In the Caddy."

Bear turned to the driver. "Dimitri, why didn't you run?"

"Thought the piece of shit was gonna push us over the wall and down the cliff. And a tour guide always goes down with his ship."

✦ ✦ ✦

Eunice and Lily were surprised to find Vinny waiting for them. He was seated on the delicate art deco chair in the elevator alcove on their deck. Its fan-shaped back scalloped around his head and shoulders. He looked like a thug on the half shell.

"Vinny! I thought you were with Bear. You were taking Ric ... ah, ridiculous hikes together." Eunice wound down, placing her hand over her mouth.

Lily looked around but saw no one within ear shot.

"This was true, Miss Eunice," Vinny said, standing in respect. "I was with Bear. But ez not true now. Now I am with you. To protect you."

"Protect me? Why ever do you need to protect me?"

"Because Signore Bear -"

Eunice interrupted. "You mean the shamus with the gloom of a Seattle night."

Oh no! Here she goes again.

Lily, in fact all of them, knew that Eunice loved to burst into film noir-speak when an investigation was afoot. But it would confuse the crap out of the mobster. "Um, Vinny, the Juneau authorities are in our cabin, waiting for us. We will be right as rain with the law all around us. Not to worry. Go get yourself some lunch, and I'll call when they're finished. We won't leave the cabin without telling you, okay?"

Vinny's face was a map of emotions, finally landing on the route to happy. "Ez good, Miss Lily. Thank you. You are very kind woman."

I'm not your mother-in-law yet, Buster. Easy on the nicey, nicey crap.

She smiled back at him. Even before her daughter started mooning over the man, Lily had been fond of him. Scared shitless of his weaponry, maybe. But fond.

A railing ran the length of the hall between all cabin doors. As the two walked to their suite, Eunice held on for support and Lily did the same walking behind her. Since the ship was tied to the dock it wasn't rocky. But neither trusted their sea legs. Or sea leg as Lily had joked to her friend.

Over her shoulder, Eunice asked, "So the private dick thinks the dolly's behind the eight ball, huh? Who's got the moxy to clip this chick?"

"Oh Eunice. You know. Men are such worriers. Bear cares about you. That's all."

Eunice stopped and turned, dropping the tec talk. "You can tell me the truth, Lily. I know Bear thinks this is about me. That someone tried to kill me at the senior center. And on board." She began walking again.

Eunice never failed to surprise Lily. Just when you thought she was flighty as her beloved birds she proved to be very down to earth. "He doesn't know it for a fact. But, yes, Bear is worried."

"That's why he came on this cruise, isn't it? Even though he didn't want to." Eunice stopped at their door.

"Don't be upset. We all love you. Besides," Lily said as she used her plastic key. "I think he's really enjoying parts of it. He beat the hell out of everyone at Rat Pack trivia after dinner last night."

"I'm sure winning a lanyard with the Celestial logo makes up for murder on the high seas."

Lily pushed the cabin door open. The two officers waiting for them inside were as different as Chihuahuas and great Danes. The woman was tightly wrapped in a size-twelve navy blue pants suit that should have been a fourteen. Her shoes were polished to a mirror-like finish and the scarf at her neck was tied into a bow with perfectly symmetrical loops. A rosy complexion clashed with orange freckles and perm-tight curls. She was maybe fifty, more muscular than plump, and looked like nobody to tangle with. Lily imagined that a female law officer in Alaska had to be a pretty tough nut.

The man was much darker, younger and steamier. He was hotter than any of the covers on her romance novels, and Lily had been reading ro-

CHAPTER SEVEN

mance for a long, long time. He was rugged and lean, smelling of wind and sea. On him, jeans and a long sleeved t-shirt looked shockingly erotic. This man must have broken hearts from Ketchikan to Prudhoe Bay.

Lily had to chortle inside. The Latin's Ranch ladies had missed a hunky law enforcement officer ever since Jo Keegan's long time partner Clay had left the scene in less than happy circumstances. She'd have to get a picture of this guy to send home to Aurora. Or maybe just keep for herself.

Lady Law shook hands with both women. She'd looked tough at first, but her blue eyes flashed with ill-concealed humor. "I'm Lulu Maxwell. Everyone calls me Max. And this is Logan Worth. He works for me although he'll tell you it's the other way around."

"You can call me Boss if you want, but most people just call me Logan." The power of his smile damn near blasted Lily and Eunice into the next cabin.

Lily did their introductions. "We're Eunice Taylor and Lily Gilbert. You can call us Eunice and Lily. I take it you're with the sheriff's department?"

"Not in Alaska. Don't have sheriffs here since we don't have counties," Max answered handing over her ID.

"We're ABI. Alaska Bureau of Investigations which is part of the State Troopers. Major Crimes Unit." Logan supplied his own credentials.

"*The first response in the last frontier,*" Max said, drawing air quotes with her fingers. "That's our motto. Sounds like you two ladies have been through a bad time. Please have a seat."

Alita's body was gone and the room had been straightened. Lily assumed crime scene investigators had come and gone. Or maybe not. Investigation on a cruise ship might not rival big city standards. She sat on the sofa next to Eunice and tried not to stare at the spot where the body had been.

There was a slight knock on the door and Logan answered it. A young man who had not yet outgrown acne slouched in. He spoke to no one, but sat next to Lily and placed a fingerprint kit on the coffee table. Max said, "We need your prints, ladies, both of you. Assuming you don't object."

"You think one of us did this?" Eunice asked as the technician went to work, gently inking Lily's fingers.

"Oh no. Not at all. We just need elimination prints to separate yours from others we found in this cabin."

As the two officers pulled up chairs from the dining table and faced the two women, Lily asked, "What will happen to Alita, I mean to her body?"

"Well, at the moment, she's in the ship's morgue."

"Cruise ships have morgues?"

"Yes, ma'am, they do," Max said. "She'll be there until we figure out jurisdiction issues. Death on a cruise ship, one that's a murder, can be investigated by the cruise company, the U.S. Coast Guard, the FBI, or the state who owns the waters where the murder took place." The technician gave Lily a cloth to wipe her fingers then he circled around to Eunice.

"How confusing," she said while complying with the technician.

"You better believe it," Max said, with a shake of her head and a "Phew." Her curls were so tight not one of them bounced but stayed stiff as little soldiers at attention. "Especially when everyone would rather keep a low profile regarding demise at sea. The cruise companies can apply a lot of pressure to, ah, let things go without a lot of turmoil."

"We'll start the investigation but we may not be the department that finishes it since you'll move on in a couple days," added Logan the Devastating.

"But that's our problem to worry about. We shouldn't bother you with it," Max said. "So let's do the important stuff. Why don't you tell us about Alita."

Lily explained their relationship with the aide, and Eunice told the officers why they were all on the ship. Lily felt wary of saying too much. These two cops were likable, sympathetic, reassuring, easy to talk to. That was so much more dangerous than good cop, bad cop when a person was trying to avoid a topic or two. Topics like knowing who the murderer was. Or knowing his carcass had been dumped overboard by their other aide Rick who had now disappeared. Lily could only hope these cops were profiling Eunice and her as charming but innocent old know-nothings. At the moment, she felt that wasn't far from the truth.

A knock at the door interrupted them. Logan went to answer, moving smooth as a big cat on the prowl.

Alejandro came bounding in carrying a large silver tray on his shoulder. When he set it down, it dwarfed the coffee table between the investigators and investigatees. "I thought you might like coffee or tea. And a few snacks for sustenance." He stared darts at the officers then smiled at Lily and Eunice. "Are my ladies all right?"

CHAPTER SEVEN

"We're fine, Alejandro. We'll let you know if we need anything else," Eunice answered. He arranged the tray, removed the cover from a plate of finger sandwiches, fluffed napkins across each lap and left only after giving the officers a Filipino version of a stink eye. The finger printer, finished with his task, left at the same time.

The cops laughed. "That steward likes you two."

"It's his job," Eunice said with a shrug.

"No, you can tell. He really likes you. You must be good to him."

"Easy to be. He works hard."

Then swift as a dart, Max dropped the smile and shot them with a question. "Who knew Alita would be in this room last night?"

No more chit chat.

Lily felt on the defense again. "I ... we ... don't know. It's no secret that it's her room."

"The ship security people say you didn't know when she came in last evening. Is that right?"

"Never saw or heard a thing." Both women shook their heads emphatically.

"But she was your aide wasn't she? Wasn't she here to help you get to bed?"

"Oh! Well -" Eunice began.

"She'd been in earlier to help us, yes," Lily cut in. "But then she'd gone out again. When we found her this morning, we thought maybe somebody broke in to rob us and ..."

"... and Alita interrupted a burglar." Eunice batted her remaining eyelashes.

"That's a lot to happen without you hearing," Logan said.

"We were in the other room," Lily said, the hairs on the back of her neck beginning to prickle.

"Wonder why she didn't cry out for your help," Max said, eyeing the plate of finger sandwiches.

Eunice and Lily looked at each other. Eunice said, "Well, we're old, you see. Don't hear like we used to. In fact, if you could both just speak a bit louder ..."

"Yep. Sleep like logs. That's us," Lily agreed.

"Did the burglar take anything?" Max lifted the corner of a piece of bread revealing a green paste underneath.

"Um, well no. Probably he got scared after he did the deed, and he left right away."

"Funny. What with you so deep asleep and all," muttered Max turning her eyes back to Lily who felt the burn.

"We'll leave that for now," Logan said. "Who else has been in here?"

"You mean since the cruise began? Well, there's the steward, of course. Plus Charlie and Frankie and Bear and ..."

Lily was saved by another knock at the door.

"Grand Central," Logan muttered as he opened the door again.

"Out of the way, young'un," said the tired PI as he *kachunked* past the cop. "I'm aiming for that easy chair." With that, Bear crashed the party.

CHAPTER EIGHT

Case Notes
May 14, 8 p.m.

Bear's timing was perfect when he hauled his carcass into our suite and deposited it in the easy chair. I was tired of tap dancing around the state troopers' questions, no longer sure what was safe to say. Wish I could have talked privately with Bear before the inquisition continued. Turns out Officers Max and Logan were ahead of me anyway. They had a secret of their own.

"Ah, if it isn't Alvin 'Bear' Jacobs, the retired Private Investigator," Max said when the overstuffed chair enveloped the big man. "Pleasure to meet you."

"How'd you know who I am?" He might be an old griz, but Bear cocked his head like a pup.

"Got a call about you and your cohorts from a Deputy Sheriff Josephine Keegan in Washington state," Max grinned at him. "Another sharp lady detective, I'd say. We're just everywhere these days."

"Oh yeah?"

"Yeah. Seems Keegan got a call from a Jessica Winslow, manager of the ... " Logan paused to consult his notes. "Latin's Ranch Adult Family Home. This Jessica told her you were involved in another murder."

"The operative word being another," Max added before plopping one of the finger sandwiches from the tea tray into her mouth.

"Oh yeah?" Bear said again.

What a conversationalist. I'm just saying.

Logan continued. "Keegan admitted you're the real deal. A bona fide investigator. Annoying as crap, but talented."

Bear rumbled something indecipherable.

Max swallowed then said, "She said you'd deceive us every step of the way if you found it in your best interest. Added that it wasn't just you. That Lily here, is your assistant. And Eunice an operative. Along with Charlie Barker." Max peered inside another sandwich, then moved on to a different one.

Apparently Keegan hadn't mentioned Frankie and Vinny. Glad to hear Cupcake has some discretion. Just as well not to sic the mob on the forty-ninth state.

For a while, Eunice, Bear and I zipped our lips. We passed the sandwich plate and played a staring game at the officers, at each other, at the spot where Alita had died, at our cuticles, at the art on the suite's walls. Finally, Bear began to talk. Eunice and I were off the hook.

Here's the stuff he said, best as I can remember.

Eunice was a supporter of the Protective Association of the Short-Tailed Albatross which was headquartered here in Juneau. She was to receive the Arctic Angel award, and we were all on this cruise to support her. Before we boarded the ship, a woman was murdered by a hawk-nosed man at the senior center where we go to experience quality social time. The quality is usually better than getting picked off in the parking lot (Bear didn't say that ... I'm just adding it now).

The senior center victim may have been mistaken for Eunice since they both wore similar shawls that day. No proof of that. But coincidence isn't Bear's cup of tea. Or glass of Alaskan ale as the case may be. Last night, on day three of the cruise, Alita was murdered here in this suite. Maybe the guy who tried for Eunice before the cruise was trying again. Or maybe a thief got on in Ketchikan, ended up killing Alita and escaped in Juneau (of course, Bear knew this wasn't true).

CHAPTER EIGHT

Now this last bit? Eunice and I hadn't been aware this had happened until right that moment: Charlie, Frankie and Bear took the private tour that Eunice had booked, and someone tried to kill them.

Lily Gilbert, Gobsmacked Assistant to PI Bear Jacobs

"What?" Lily exclaimed.

"Is Frankie okay?" Eunice gasped.

"Charlie?"

"They're fine. Shaken, of course, but okay other than a couple bruises. The ship is locating a new wheel chair and walker for them. Theirs look like Rube Goldberg machines."

Logan made a call while Bear explained why he had been with Charlie and Frankie in Dimetri's car. The big man used admirable upper body English to portray how the Humvee had bashed them, how its driver wore a ski mask and a down black parka with no distinguishing marks. "Guess Ski Mask panicked after seeing all those tourists taking photos."

"They weren't just taking pictures," Logan said, momentarily breaking away from the call. "911 received eight calls from them to report the occurrence."

Bear said, "The uniforms who caught the call didn't think they'd have much trouble finding the vehicle. It's pretty unique in an area with almost no roads. But I don't know that it will matter. Chances are it was stolen just for this escapade."

Logan listened a little longer to the phone then said to Bear, "You're right. They got a call from an owner missing a Humvee." He clicked off his phone. "Hey, Max, we should go look into this before the office screws it up."

Max nodded and stood. "We'll get back to you soon. Lots of questions for you to play dodge ball with." She softened when she turned to the ladies. "I know you're sad. And probably scared. We'll find the guy. You'll be okay."

Bear held up a paw to stop them. "Here's more you should know. I saw that damn Humvee on the dock before we left on the tour. Our driver Dimitri had been holding a sign for Eunice Taylor. I'm thinking Ski Mask walked around the dock - without the mask, of course - waiting to see Eunice get off the ship, but instead saw that sign. Ski Mask assumed Eunice would be in Dimitri's Highlander."

"How do you know that?" Max asked.

"I don't. But Ski Mask thought it would be a woman in the car. Not Charlie, Frankie and me."

"Anything else to tell us about the guy?" The sharp edge in Logan's voice irritated Bear.

Better not think I'm toothless, kid.

"Well, yes. I didn't say Ski Mask was a guy. You assumed it. The voice was too low, like it was exaggerated. An impersonation. I think Ski Mask was a woman whose voice is husky enough to let her get away with it."

✦ ✦ ✦

The cops were gone. Everyone from Latin's Ranch was back on board ... everyone except Rick. Vinny escorted Frankie to his cabin for a much-needed nap before dinner. The rest were gathered in a tight circle of lounge chairs for privacy as well as the comfort of being close together. In the corner of the Star Power Bar a pianist tinkled the kind of old standards that Bear knew word for word. He hummed Stormy Weather between sips of his ale, and he listened to the others chatter.

"But why does anybody want to kill me?" Eunice asked. Bear could tell she was more pissed off than frightened. What he liked best about the technicolor-wardrobed, glitz-encrusted, cosmetic-enhanced woman was her core of bedrock.

"Don't worry, Eunice. We'll take care of you," Charlie said. It made Bear wince. Charlie so rarely could detect what a woman was really feeling.

"Thanks, Charlie. But I'm not incapacitated, you know. I'm not a waif lost on the sea of life. I've learned a few self defense moves myself." Eunice leaped up, shrieked, "BACK OFF!" and struck out in the general direction

CHAPTER EIGHT

of an imaginary nose. As she reclaimed her seat, several other passengers moved to the far end of the lounge as if the pianist might protect them.

"Who all knows you're here, Eunice? On the ship ... getting an award?" asked Lily. Bear was pleased his eWatson asked good questions and hoped Charlie would button his lip.

"You mean who knew before we boarded? Well, let's see. All of you, of course. People at the senior center. Everyone at the Curl Up 'n Dye. My ophthalmologist and her staff. The -"

"Okay. Pretty much the entire free world," Charlie cut in.

Damnation.

Bear shot him a warning glance while Eunice snapped, "Well, there was no reason to keep it a secret."

Charlie didn't take the hint. "What about PASTA, Eunice? Did they know how you were getting here?"

"Of course. That's why we planned the ceremony for today. Because the ship would be here. I guess I'll get the award tomorrow now. I'm waiting to hear from Dr. Flavenmire about when and where."

Charlie knit his eyebrows. "Have you met the good doctor? Could he be the hawk-nosed man?"

"Well, no and no, Charlie. I haven't met him, but I've talked to him since the hawk-nosed man was ... ah ... departed. So he can hardly be dead."

"Yeah, that's true. Okay, no more guessing games for me," Charlie said with a shrug. "Pushed my brain as far as it will go, at least 'til I have another Golden Cadillac. Anyone else ready?" He turned toward the bar, then stopped. "My oh my, just look who's over there." He picked up as much speed as an old man in a wheel chair on thick carpet could muster.

"That's the heart throb he met in the Ketchikan saloon?" Lily asked.

"That's the one." Bear said.

They all watched as Charlie did a wheelie next to her chair. Bear thought she seemed glad to see him. At least she didn't shriek, "Get lost."

"He can be as annoying as a yapping dog," Eunice muttered. "But if a shipboard romance is in the offing, well, here's hoping he succeeds."

Bear couldn't help but think of the problem with Charlie's nuts but he said not a word about it to the ladies.

Lily turned their attention back to business. "Attempts have been made by two different people. Hawk Nose and Ski Mask, who may or may not have been a woman. You think this is a professional hit of some kind?"

"Far from it," Bear answered. "Amateurs. Nobody makes three attempts on the life of one - you should pardon the phrase, Eunice - elderly woman and fails three times. Damn near impossible to be that bad at it."

"You figure it's related to PASTA, don't you?" Eunice asked.

Bear hadn't wanted to hurt her by accusing an organization she had supported for so long. He was profoundly grateful that she'd brought up the five hundred pound gorilla all on her own. "Pretty much has to be."

"I agree," said Lily. "I'm so sorry, Eunice. But they do look suspicious."

"What do you know about Dr. Leland Flavenmire?" Bear asked.

"Nothing much, really. But he does know his birds and what is necessary to protect the Short-Tailed Albatross and other rare species. He's worked at it for years. I've always been impressed by him, at least in that way."

"Hmmm." Bear rested his elbows on the cushy chair arms and his chin on the tent created by his joined hands. "Eunice, I've known you a long time and respect your privacy. But I wonder if I could ask you about your background now."

She did not give him an immediate answer. Instead, she finished her wine and motioned to a waiter for another. "I've always believed, Bear, that the reason you, Lily, Charlie and I bonded so completely has to do with the fact that life started anew for the four of us when we met. None of us dwell on our past. We befriended each other after we'd lived the richer years of our existence. We're not hampered by knowing what we all have lost."

"I understand, Eunice. I feel the same," Bear said with a nod. His Latin's Ranch friends valued who he was. They didn't miss who he had been.

"But in this case, I think it's wise to tell you whatever you need to know. I must understand whether I am in any way responsible for Alita's death. So please, ask your questions and I will answer."

"I know you and your husband were well off. What was the source of that money?"

"He wasn't well off, Bear. He was filthy rich. I never felt the money was essential, just one of his pleasant characteristics. Like his laugh or his sense of fair play. The family fortune goes way back to property purchased

CHAPTER EIGHT

by his forefather under the Homestead Act, sometime in the 1800s, but I don't know the exact date. I'll look it up if it's important to you. Now let's see," Eunice stopped speaking. The features of her face got all squinty as though she were forcing her brain to emit a buried memory. With her spiky hair she looked like a hedgehog in deep thought.

At last, she succeeded. "That's it! The family surname that far back was Blankenship. Blankenship the Original got 160 acres on the Olympic Peninsula and, on his death, his widow got the adjacent 160. Through time the family bought more, and through marriage, the name changed to Taylor. In the early going, they mostly farmed, if I remember how my husband told it to me. With expansion of the railroads, they became land barons with lumber and mining interests."

Lily said, "Sounds like they had a green thumb for raising money as well as crops."

"Oh, my yes," Eunice nodded. "My husband, Thomas, inherited the whole kit and caboodle since he was the oldest living male at the time of his father's death. At least I imagine the women didn't count if there was any other option. But Thomas was a bit of a black sheep. Had more than a few family fights through the years until he broke away from the rest of them altogether. He still leased vast stretches, but always replenished forest through the years. Money grew on trees. Literally."

Eunice stopped and sipped her wine. Bear watched her dear wrinkled face, her earrings dangling multi-colored sparkly things. He could see that her eyes, usually so clear, seemed unfocused on anything in the room as she stared into the long ago. A Mona Lisa smile crossed her lips. Bear assumed that Thomas had entered the room where she kept the best of her memories.

He was proved right when she returned to the conversation. She'd been with Thomas. "I was a second wife to Thomas. But I like to believe I was not only his last but his best. He was a very wealthy man long before I met him. That wealth passed to me at his death. I contribute a lot to environmental causes now in hopes of making up for any mistakes his family may have made along the way."

"So the money you provide to PASTA comes from that?"

"Yes. I have a charitable trust in place. It pays out enough annually to keep PASTA up and running. At my demise, the trust goes to PASTA with the organization as trustee." She stopped for another long sip of the wine. "Are you thinking Dr. Flavenmire is a little too eager for my demise?"

"Well," Bear said. "It's a possibility. But something feels off with that, too. There's more to it."

"What do you mean?" Lily asked.

"Let's assume Hawk Nose worked for PASTA. That he failed to kill Eunice at the senior center. He knew Eunice was taking this cruise, so he booked passage to make a second try."

"But he screwed up again." Eunice said.

"Big time. He comes in the room, finds Alita instead of you, kills her and takes the brooch. Maybe he's a thief as well as a killer. Or maybe he thought he'd divert attention from his real goal by stealing the thing."

"And, of course, there's a chance it's the truth, that he was just a thief. Everyone saw the brooch on Eunice that night. It must have looked tempting. Maybe he hadn't been the person who killed a woman at the senior center ... just a passenger looking for an easy mark." Lily's mind was working the problem as she talked. "But if so, everything should have been over and done with yesterday when he disappeared overboard."

"That's right. Instead, another attempt was made today, made on the Highlander that was supposed to be squiring Eunice." Bear used his midriff as a table to tap his fingers. "So another person is involved. If Hawk Nose was working with someone else at PASTA, they might not know he died on board. They'd think his mission was a success. They wouldn't have set up a third attempt here in Juneau. There just wouldn't have been time or a reason."

Lily leaned forward toward her friends and lowered her voice. "Unless somebody was his partner here on the ship and called ahead to tell another partner that Hawk Nose was missing and Eunice was alive. That's at least three bad guys. One of whom may be a bad gal."

"Right," Bear nodded. "There's a piece or two missing, ladies. Need more information. But we'll get to the truth."

"Hope we get to it before they get to me." Eunice said then drained her glass.

Bear wished he could spare her the fear she concealed so well. "I know you're anxious, Eunice. You have every reason to be. But you have a lot of

CHAPTER EIGHT

friends looking out for you. Including a couple of Alaska cops who trust Keegan enough to be more help than hindrance."

Lily said. "They do seem a little less possessive than others I've known when they're on a case. I wonder if all the jurisdiction issues cool their enthusiasm."

"It was true back in my day. Staties, sheriffs, state bureaus and federal. All jealous as hell of each other. Add in the cruise investigators and you have a real mixed bag. They have too many cases as is to give a rat's ass about one that's overcrowded."

"You're counting on that working for us, aren't you?"

Bear scratched at a collar bone where his deep blue suspender crossed it. "Can't hurt. If a hound's not sure the bone will be his, he may not dig too deep for it." He had a hard time thinking of Max as a dog. But to be fair, he added, "He or she."

Dinner chimes interrupted them.

"It's time to eat, ladies. Glad it's smart casual night, whatever the hell that is."

"I think it means jeans with no knee holes will be okay."

They got up and stood still until their old joints felt loose enough to move.

"First thing in the morning, I need to tell the troopers that Rick is missing," Bear said. "I've let it go as long as possible. If they discover for themselves we're missing another aide, they'll know we've been deceiving them."

Eunice donned her ditsy self once more. "Whatever do you mean, we've been deceiving them? I'd never do such a thing." Her bracelet charms tinkled as she shook a finger at him before they turned toward the dining room.

CHAPTER NINE

Case Notes
May 15, 7 a.m.

It's going to be a busy day so just a short note before my morning stretches. Last night's dinner was a tranquil affair. Frankie had room service, and Vinny stayed with him. Charlie didn't show. I assume he was in the bar with his new sweetie pie. If I wasn't already up to here with intrigue, I'd give more thought to what she sees in him. I'd say she's a fair amount younger, and let's face it, Charlie's best qualities aren't immediately obvious. But I guess widows on cruise ships don't have a lot of choice, so that probably explains that.

Of course, neither Alita nor Rick were with us, so our table for eight only had three occupants. Bear's right. Our dwindling number is getting obvious. We told the waiter and his assistant that we thought our colleagues were all dining in Juneau for the evening since we would be in port all night. That seemed enough to stave off their curiosity although they probably wondered who the hell would choose a meal in Juneau over the Celestial Superstar. I must say, the tiger shrimp kebobs with mango-lime relish were outstanding. Even Aurora would have been impressed.

We tucked into our suite early because we were so very tired. Eunice hand washed some dainties while I hung up our clothes and got out what we'd need in the morning. Removing this prosthesis is still new to me and doing it without an aide is no picnic. I'm worried I won't

CHAPTER NINE

be able to get it back on. But I'll manage. Eunice will help. If not, Alejandro. Guess I needn't dwell on how much we miss Alita.
Eunice heard from Dr. Flavenmire late in the evening. He had managed to cancel the award ceremony and reset it for today. But he had not been able to rearrange all the honored guests. Nor could he rebook the lobby of the state capitol building for the ceremony. In fact, the best he could do was one o'clock at the Howlin' Wolf saloon. He told Eunice that it wouldn't be as grand as he'd hoped. But the Howlin' Wolf did have a collection of handsome beer steins, and they promised to make hors d'oeuvres fresh in the morning. "Some of those little weenies in dough and meatballs on toothpicks," Eunice added, chuckling when she told me what Flavenmire had said.
"Who do you suppose the B-list of guests in Juneau might be?" I asked. "The assistant deputy mayor? Sanitation workers?"
"Well, someone from the chamber of commerce, for sure. They always show up when there's free food. And at least one person from the State Fisheries, what with fishing rights being tangled up with the Short-Tailed Albatross. Proprietor of the local birder store, maybe? The Howlin' Wolf hostess? I know! Dimitri, since he's driving us to the event. He's borrowing a vehicle since his Highlander is out of commission."
We're all going to go together. We're not leaving Eunice on her own until this whole damn thing is straightened out.

- Lily Gilbert, Social Assistant to PI Bear Jacobs

After dinner, Bear left a message for the Alaska troopers to come early in the morning; he had something to tell them. Then he called Latin's Ranch to ask Jessica if she'd send Will along with Chrissie.

"You mean Rick just left you?" Jessica sounded appalled. "Bear, I flat out don't believe he'd do that."

"No, Jess. He had good reasons. Can't tell you everything at the moment. Cell phone and all. But we need Will to fill in. I'll tell you everything as soon as I can."

"Bear, are you in trouble?" she asked. Jessica always played fair and square with him. She fretted, of course, but in the end, she believed he knew what he was doing. He was not proud of withholding information from her. And he never wanted to push her too far. If she ever booted him off the Ranch, he'd literally have no other place to go. Poor and disabled, he'd have to stand on a curb, hoping Waste Management would haul him away.

"I won't lie to you, Jessica. Things could be better. But we're surrounded by law enforcement. And, of course, Vinny." He nearly added "Trust me" then thought better of it.

"Okay then. I'll get Will on the plane along with Chrissie. Guess I can take care of her kids. But an ass-burning lecture is awaiting you back home. All of you." She hung up on him causing him to smile. Bear appreciated a woman with attitude.

As he was buttoning on his pajama top, his cell rang. He picked it up, read the name and answered, "Good to hear from you, Cupcake."

She sighed, probably at the nickname, then spoke. "Just checking in, Bear. You okay? Lily?"

He told her they'd be better when help arrived, that things were harder than necessary without aides. They all liked to think of themselves as completely independent, but they all knew they weren't.

Old age is a real bitch.

"We talked with Alita's parents," Keegan said. "Your Deputy Logan Worth requested we tell them about her death."

"Wondered who'd inherit that job."

"Yeah. Lots of parties if they cared to get involved. Alaska, the cruise line, the feds ... anyway, Alita's parents live in our jurisdiction so we drew the short straw."

Bear knew she didn't mean to sound crass. No officer craved that part of an investigation, the sitting with a parent mourning the loss of a child.

"Hard." It was a major speech of commiseration for Bear.

"Yeah. But you know Brandon? The new guy you met at Latin's Ranch? He did a great job with them. Better than me. Maybe he'll make a good partner one of these days. Can't be worse that the last one."

It was the first reference he'd heard her make to the loss of Clay in a long time. Maybe she was healing. Seemed like grief was a raincloud that they

CHAPTER NINE

all were under so much of the time.

She asked the question he dreaded. "Bear, is this related to the murder at the senior center?"

"I don't know, Jo. I don't. But I have my suspicions."

When they said good-night, Bear put his phone on the nightstand and laid down on the bed. He wanted to save Rick, or at least give him time to disappear. But he hated the idea of pissing off Cupcake by being less than truthful. Like Jessica, Deputy Detective Josephine Keegan was important to his wellbeing. Most other law enforcement officials would consider him no more than a wearisome old nuisance. While Keegan might think the same from time to time, she also valued his abilities as an investigator. She gave him respect that kept his big old brain from going out to pasture.

Bear was in the *Superstar Diner* when Max and Logan showed up to meet him at eight am. They took advantage of another free buffet breakfast. "I could get used to this," Max said as she buttered a third tropical fruit pancake. Hers was the kind of round little body than could surge beyond plump at any moment.

Their table neighbored one of the huge windows that surrounded the buffet and eating area which was about a third the length of the entire ship. This morning, sprigs of tiny blue forget-me-not flowers were in crystal bud vases on every table. Alaska's state flower, Max had told him.

Where the hell does the ship come up with stuff like that? A garden below decks?

The delicate touch of color was at odds with the view of deep green water, working tugs, fishing boats, seaplanes and floating logs in the harbor. Bear knew that the view from the other side would show passengers disembarking for another morning of tours and souvenirs where buses and shops lined up along the dock.

"What's up, Mr. Jacobs?" said Logan. Bear wondered if the cop was aware of the stir he made among the womenfolk at the other tables.

Couple of the menfolk, too, for that matter.

"Call me Bear. I need to tell you that we're missing our aide."

"You mean Alita Aarons?" Max looked up, pancake bite suspended on her fork. Bear saw the pity in her eyes as she looked at him. This cop may be tough, but she couldn't hide anything in those baby blues.

"I'm not going senile, officer. I know Alita is gone. I mean Rick Peters."

"Damn inconvenient," whined Charlie, wheeling up to the table trailed by a waiter carrying his breakfast for him. "Damn inconvenient to have your damn aide disappear in the middle of a damn cruise that's supposed to be fun but is turning into a damn lot of work for someone old and fragile as me. Damn it." Charlie had a tendency to lay it on too thick, especially when he was truly upset. The Latin's Ranch gang were all grieving at the loss of the young man who'd provided for them so long.

The cops both looked dumbfounded until Charlie finally settled down. Then Max asked, "You have not one aide but two?"

"Had," Bear answered.

"You had two aides on this ship, and you said nothing to us?" Logan frowned. Some of the women in the diner looked like they could beat Bear for upsetting the young man.

"It wasn't relevant. We'd only lost one the last time we talked. But last night Rick didn't show to help us with our nightly routine."

"Is that all of them? Or do each of you have an aide of your own? Are aides just going to keep popping out of the woodwork?" Logan snapped then compressed his lips which squared his jaw all the more.

Bear truly wished that Chrissie and Will hadn't shown up at that exact moment. Chrissie rushed to him and encircled his ample self with her arms. "Oh Bear!" she cried. "We took the red eye. Got here as soon as we could."

Will shook Charlie's hand, patted his shoulder, and said, "I may not be as experienced as Rick, but I'll give it all I got. Whatever you guys need, just ask."

"Just don't embalm us."

"Then you better keep breathing," Will said with a smile.

Chrissie cut in. "The ship is confused about us, especially Will. They don't seem to know they have another passenger missing, that you need to replace both aides. They told us to come here while they look into it. So we have to wait, but I should get to Lily and Eunice as soon as I can. How they're doing without Alita ... oh, Bear, how will any of us do without Alita? Or Rick." Chrissie continued to hug the big man.

"EXCUSE US," Logan raised his voice above the reunion. "Could we please have a little quiet before I call your Deputy Keegan to come yell at you?"

CHAPTER NINE

"Maybe she could arrange for a firing squad," Max added. Bear figured Logan was actually pissed off, but he could see the glee in her eyes. *This lady detective. I like her.*

"Okay, you two. Go get some breakfast, then grab a seat," Bear said, extracting himself from Chrissie's embrace.

"Yes. And be careful. Aides have a habit of disappearing," Max added as the two left for the buffet.

Logan felt none of the mirth that was tickling Max. His eyes shot arrows at Bear. "What the, excuse my French, fuck is going on?"

Bear decided to play the handicapped card. "Well officers, maybe you have noticed that we are physically challenged, each in our own way. And we are not merely AARP-qualified but actual *senior* senior citizens. Being without aides is not just uncomfortable. It is life threatening."

"Oh the pain, oh the sorrow, oh the ..."

"Knock it off, you old bullshitter," Max said, cutting Charlie's keening short. "We get it. You needed replacements."

"But how did they get here so soon?" Logan asked. "Didn't you just miss the other aide last night?"

Charlie's eyes opened wide as a lemur. "Ah, good questions ..."

"When Rick didn't show, we didn't have any way to go look for him. I called home and said we needed two aides instead of one from Latin's Ranch. Like Chrissie just said, they caught a red eye. Easy from Seattle to Juneau." He played the handicapped card again. "None of us likes putting our care in the hands of strangers. You can understand that."

"Okay. Yeah, sure. Since a deputy sheriff in Washington vouches for you, we're gonna play along. But don't hand us a reason to change our minds, or we'll come Bear hunting. Logan," Max said, all amusement now gone. "Tell them what we've been up to."

Logan pushed back from the table and crossed his legs, one ankle on the opposite knee. He held his coffee cup as if warming his hands and Bear could see he was looking damn proud of himself. "We took a look at the ship's security video from the night of the murder."

Bear tightened every orifice. When Charlie started saying, "Oh shit! They -" Bear delivered a pinch to the bean-spiller's thigh just above the knee. Charlie shut down with an "Eeep!" It sounded like he'd stepped on a squirrel's tail.

"Security tape, huh? Tell me," Bear said. He casually broke apart a warm croissant and slowly buttered it.

"Not much to see outside. Just views along the sides of the ship and a whole lot of ocean. Except around midnight. That's when a guy goes overboard on the starboard side."

"Oh yeah?"

"Oh yeah. Appears to be from a cabin balcony that's down the hall from the cabin where Alita Aarons was murdered."

"Get a look at who it was?"

"Tape's not that clear. But the ship's getting us the names of who was registered to cabins in that area." Max stopped a waiter who was circulating with orange juice.

"What is clear is that the guy didn't look like he took a dive. Maybe not just a guy, but a dead guy. A body thrown overboard. It would take some strength to do that. Maybe the kind of strength a male aide might have," Logan said.

"Ah aide, huh? Or maybe a stevedore. Or an ice road trucker," Charlie shot back. "Rick is a good guy. He'd never do anything like that." He crossed his arms and glowered.

"Anything on any interior tapes?" Bear asked. Everything hinged on whether the inside corridor tape would show Rick and Hawk Nose in the hall or Bear going from cabin to cabin. "One in the hall, maybe?"

"Well, that's the thing," Max said. "Most ships don't have corridor cameras. Not required by law. Besides, a lot of corridors zig or zag. They're not straight enough for cameras to work anyway."

She paused to chug her juice. Logan stared at Bear.

Finally, the big man was forced to ask, "What about this ship?"

"The *Celestial Superstar* has no corridor cameras. So we have no tapes to tell the tale if there's a tale to tell."

Bear relaxed his body but not his mind. "Surprising. What a shame."

"The ship leaves late afternoon today. This morning, we'll interview passengers and crew about what they may have seen or heard."

"And we'll straighten out the ship's office regarding your replacement aides. We're not assholes, Bear. We know you need them." The troopers got ready to leave. Max pushed her chair back.

CHAPTER NINE

Bear stopped her. "You won't really know who's missing until everyone's supposed to be back on board at five."

"Right. Since the ship was in port last night, not everyone checked back in." This time she stood and Logan joined her.

"So Rick may still appear, making apologies after an all night bender." Bear nodded. "Anything could happen."

"Yep. In fact, a woman called to say her boyfriend is missing. Didn't come back last night when she expected him. Maybe he's on that bender with Rick. Or maybe he's the one who went overboard."

"We're going to talk to her now," Logan said. "But we'll join you at Eunice's ceremony this afternoon."

A woman reporting a missing person? Now what the hell is that about? Bear decided he might need another cup of caffeine.

✦ ✦ ✦

Vinny was just back from the ship's gym when Sylvia caught him on the phone.

"You sound out of breath," she said. Was he breathing hard for her? Would he ever open the neck of her blouse and run his hand down her long throat to ...

"Yes. I work out. Now I go to shower."

She imagined his chest naked and slick with musk, her tongue at his ...

Stop it! Stop it!

She held an icy glass of Diet Coke to her hot crimson cheek. "Ah, I called to ask you what's going on. Mom told me that Chrissie is replacing Alita. But she's being her normal obstructive self and saying nothing more. Jessica is saying nothing more. So I know it's something more. Plenty more."

"But my love, I thought you call to talk of us, of our future, not of the old ones."

"Yes, but when I talk to Lily -"

"I dream of you and the night that we will first be together."

"I mean she never tells me -"

"How you will be in my arms and we will discover a heaven on earth in each other."

"Vinny, I -"

"You must tell me you will be mine and we will marry."

It was always the same. She wanted rapture. He wanted commitment. It was only after they said good-bye that she realized he hadn't told her a thing about Lily's well-being. She'd just been so damn distracted by her own chemistry.

Or had the Italian stallion actually out-smarted her?

Eunice was paying for the cruise, but Bear just couldn't see giving in to the jacked up rates in the ship's internet room. Alejandro showed him where the crew used the internet when they were off the ship in Juneau. He had some research to do and rather fancied the tiny store that had six computer stations between shelves stocked with foods for Filipinos, Indonesians, Russians and other cruise cultures. All around him, he heard crew members chattering in their own languages on their phones to loved ones back home. He wondered what the store owners did during the long winter months when cruise ships were partying in warmer climes.

He Googled and Binged, searched and scanned. In time, he found what he was looking for. He decided he'd tell Eunice what he'd come up with after the ceremony when they'd have time to talk it through. Besides, he saw no reason for her to fret any more than she already was.

He frisked himself for his cell phone and called Lily. "Pick me up at the International Market on your way to Howlin' Wolf, okay? Dimitri will know where it is."

"You're sure to see us coming."

"Whadaya mean?"

"Two armored Mercedes limos. Vinny at the wheel of one, Dimitri at the other."

"Where did Juneau come up with those?"

CHAPTER NINE

"Not sure Juneau had anything to do with it. Frankie did it. When I asked he just answered, 'Professional courtesy.' Don't think I'll ask any more."

Bear snickered. An escort from the Alaska troopers would have been good enough. But it couldn't hold a candle to special delivery by the mob. Frankie's little dove would arrive in over protected style.

When the two ferocious hunks of shiny black metal purred to a stop in front of the store, Vinny motioned him into the front passenger side of the first one. Once settled, Bear turned and saw three identical women in the back seat. Well, at least three women in identical flowered scarves, peasant blouses and loose print skirts. As he peered closer, he saw the three were Lily, Eunice and Chrissie.

"Chrissie was taking no chances," Lily said, revealing no emotion whatsoever. "She went out shopping early."

"Bought three identical outfits," Eunice said. Her voice couldn't avoid a bit of piqué. "Forced us to wear them."

Chrissie crossed her arms and snapped, "Canes, too, so Eunice and I match Lily. Maybe a little too Russian peasant for modern tastes, okey-dokey, but if a gunman is out there, he won't be able to pick Eunice out of the crowd."

Bear stared at one then the next, then the next. "Did you consider that he might just shoot all three of you?"

The three women remained mute, their faces half hidden under the enormous babushkas.

Finally, Chrissie said, "Crap."

✦ ✦ ✦

When the Latin's Ranch gang arrived at the Howlin' Wolf Saloon, it was still an hour before the ceremony was to begin. Everyone had agreed that an early arrival was in their best interest. As they entered through the western-themed swinging doors, Vinny peeled off to investigate any villain hidey holes in the place. Charlie wheeled straight to the bar. Eunice wanted to meet Dr. Flavenmire and discuss the PASTA program, and Bear planned to observe every guest as they arrived for the ceremony.

A hostess, dressed in a school marm look, led them toward an archway in the back. As they crossed the main room, Lily became more than aware that historical accuracy was not a bugaboo for the Howlin' Wolf decorators. The place was a tourist trap. If not, the local population of Juneau must be stuck in some bizarre time warp. The saloon's walls were imitation hand-hewn planks decorated with prospectors' rusty pans and picks, commercial fishing nets, bobbers, and life rings, sepia photos of deadly desperados and poorly clothed dames, stuffed animal heads, antique beer signs, and above it all, enormous wagon wheel chandeliers. The far end of the open room was a massive bar tended by dance hall girls and city slickers.

Lily wondered just how many anachronisms had crossed wires here. She, Chrissie and Eunice, dressed as handicapped Russian peasants, didn't even draw much of a stare from tourists at the hodgepodge of tables.

In the L off the main room, where the ceremony would be held, the decor was a little more Victorian boudoir. At least, the seats of the chairs were green velvet, Lily noticed, as the Latin's Ranch gang limped, rolled, and *ka-chunked* through the archway and into the room. There they stopped. Their attention was focused past large tables set up for guests. On a riser with a podium at the far end of the room, a large man was yelling at a little girl.

Their backs were to the Latin's Ranch group as the man ran his hands through his thick gray mane, causing it to stand at peculiar angles not unlike Einstein on a bad hair day. "Who'd have thought arranging an award for one little old lady would be such a hassle?" he bellowed.

"I don't know, Dr. Flavenmire," said the girl.

Not a little girl but a small woman, Lily realized as the pixie turned toward them. A bombshell of surprise exploded across her tiny heart-shaped face.

"Next year, I'll by God mail the Arctic Angel Award to the winner and be done with it."

"Dr. Flavenmire," the pixie yelped and tugged at the man's sleeve.

The good doctor was on a roll and paid her no mind. "Maybe I'll just say send us your money but stay the hell at home."

"Dr. Flavenmire!" She tugged again.

CHAPTER NINE

"Why are you pulling on me?" he raged. "Has everyone gone insane?"

"DR. FLAVENMIRE, WE HAVE GUESTS!" Pixie screamed, yanking until she finally turned him around.

Lily watched tremors cross his face as he tried to make sense of what he saw. His first attempt was a failure as he stared wide-eyed. "Are you Russian nesting dolls? The three of you? Here to do some damn performance? Did I book you? Who the hell are the rest of you?"

Eunice stepped forward and cooed in a soothing voice that could calm a wild horse. "Dr. Flavenmire? I'm Eunice Taylor. These are my friends. We're so glad to be here."

The man's dark brown eyes went from glum-to-gleeful in a split second, just beating out his mouth's scowl-to-smile. "Mrs. Taylor!" He bounded forward like an Alaskan malamute, one that might leap into her arms. Fortunately he stopped before colliding with her. "We're pleased you are finally here." He grabbed her hand and kissed it. "Just holding a last minute, ah, staff meeting with Heather, my research assistant." He cocked his head toward the pixie.

"Sounds like we've come at an awkward time."

"No, no, not at all, just a few nerves before the curtain goes up. We want you to have such a good time. Now then, who all is here?"

Eunice began the introductions. Meanwhile, Charlie, who had gone to the bar for a beer, rolled into the room. He pulled next to Bear and whispered, "Will you look at that snout!"

Of course, everyone heard his high pitched whisper. Lily was plenty sure that Bear, along with everyone else, was already aware of Dr. Leland Flavenmire's hawk nose. It was immense. If the man needed to blow it, the resulting trumpet would echo across the Alaskan tundra to start a caribou stampede.

Dr. Flavenmire covered his embarrassment well, assuming he had any. He touched the side of his nose in a Santa-like gesture. "Yes, it is a good sized honker. Family trait."

"Any chance you had family on our cruise?" Bear asked.

"Why yes! My brother Harlan planned to meet up with you. Did he?"

Everyone shook their heads back and forth as if observing a fast motion tennis match.

The doctor's brow gathered in a crumpled line of worry. "I expected him yesterday, but haven't heard from him. Maybe he jumped ship, ha ha."

✦ ✦ ✦

The opening pleasantries accomplished, Dr. Flavenmire told Heather to show the others to honored guest seats, then he and the three Russian dolls went off to the podium to chat about the presentation. Bear could see the nerves in Heather's demeanor as she was left staring at Will, Charlie, Frankie and Bear.

"Um, this way gentlemen," she said shyly and led them to a circular table in the corner of the room that was graced with a RESERVED sign.

"What do you do for PASTA?" Bear asked as he *kachunked* beside her. He wanted to give her a comfortable subject. Not that he was being nice. He just knew most people talked more when they were at ease. And Bear was fishing.

"Well, sir, I intern three days a week to receive credit toward my ornithology class. Today, I'm helping with the ceremony, but I mostly care for injured birds until they can be moved to sanctuaries."

"You're caring for a bunch of old injured birds here, too," Charlie remarked as the men arranged themselves around the table and parked their variety of mobility equipment.

"Dr. Flavenmire seems harried," Bear said then indicated an empty chair next to him. "Sit with us for a while."

She was so small she slipped into the chair without pulling it any further out from the table. "Well, this is important to him. Mrs. Taylor really is our Arctic Angel."

"Must be worried about that missing brother, too."

"It's not like Harlan to disappear. He's our financial guy so PASTA matters to him, too."

"Oh? Well, I'm sure he'll be okay. Probably got too full at the buffet to disembark. Just sleeping it off."

"Maybe. And I hope Mr. Flavenmire's wife shows up soon. He's not

CHAPTER NINE

been the same since she went missing last week."

Flavenmire's voice bawled her name across the room and she leaped up, a pheasant flushed from the bush. "Oops, better go see what he needs. They're setting up the appetizers now. Be sure to help yourself when it's ready. Lots of local favorites."

Bear had positioned himself back to wall so he had a full view of the entryway arch. He watched two costumed dancehall girls set up a coffee urn and bring in trays of food. Charlie whizzed over to the buffet then back to the table with a field report.

"Sure enough, there are pigs-in-blankets. But these pigs aren't pigs! They're reindeer hotdogs in blankets." As a charged up Charlie went back to scout out more details, Bear viewed a platter with a stunning variety of cold seafood wheeled in on a teacart. King crab legs and claws, shrimp, oysters and smoked salmon.

Charlie returned. "They have fireweed honey for the sourdough bread. Don't know about that. But the lingenberry tarts look good. Boy, would Aurora be amazed. Never heard of some of this stuff."

As the food arrived, so did guests. The first in the room were Vinny and Dimitri who took seats at one of the nearby tables. With them came Driver Dan. Bear chuckled. There may be no roads, but by god they had drivers. Max and Logan stayed just outside the archway, eyeing guests. Men and women in tailored suits greeted each other, shook hands, and selected seats. Rougher trade sauntered in, too. Bear wondered if a wardrobe of bib overalls, work boots and flannel wool was Juneau's idea of business casual.

As the room filled, Heather weaved her way through the guests back to Bear. "Eunice, Lily and Chrissie are going to the ladies room to change out of those Russian costumes. They'll be back before the ceremony begins." He looked up as Chrissie, Lily and Eunice left the room through a doorway at the opposite end of the room, just off the podium. Lily gave him a thumbs up ... at least he thought it was Lily. Babushkas all looked alike to him. Bear motioned to Frankie, Frankie motioned to Vinny, and Vinny worked his way toward the door at the back, following the ladies.

Charlie drew Bear's attention back to the table. "Veronica! You came!" he squeaked. Bear looked up to see the lady from the cruise ship, the one who had caused Charlie's delicate old heart to throb.

"Bear! This is Veronica!"

"How do you do?" she said in a husky voice, full of smoke and whisky. She took Bear's hand. He felt an extra pressure, an intimate pleasure, before her warm fingers parted from his paw. She was maybe fifty, with a soft lush figure as knowing as the look in her eyes and the fullness of her lips.

What in the hell does this woman see in Charlie?

"Please join us, Veronica." Charlie said, grappling from his wheelchair with the chair recently vacated by Heather.

"But first, to powder my nose."

Veronica patted his shoulder then moved away. The rocking motion of her stern launched thoughts of a thousand ships. Bear couldn't easily take his eyes away. But his brain began to work.

This woman wouldn't be interested in Charlie. Not for any reason.

Her low, husky voice suddenly sounded familiar.

The voice of Ski Mask.

Bear lurched to stand. The crowd was too thick now for him to make his way through it to the back door. He turned to the archway and called, "Max!"

She heard and looked up. She must have seen his fear.

"The ladies room! Now!"

Max exploded into motion. Logan was not far behind.

✦ ✦ ✦

Lily sat on a bench in the ladies room talking with Eunice, who was primping at the mirror over the sink. The bench was tall and hard, constructed from half rounds of logs. "Sort of a torture device for the butt," Lily pointed out. She had removed the long Russian skirt, revealing her black slacks underneath. Somehow, the flimsy material had wrapped itself around her cane and she was unwinding the miserable thing.

"No wonder Russian women aren't known for their fashion sense." Eunice said as she fluffed out her orange spikes which had bent to the will of the babushka.

CHAPTER NINE

They both froze when the bathroom door opened and they heard Max screaming from a distance, "Lily! Eunice! Get out."

But a stranger with the knife rushed in before the door swung shut. She locked the door to the bathroom as she growled in a low, rasping voice, "Which of you bitches is Eunice?" The knife in her hand dripped malice.

Eunice backed away until her legs hit the bench and she toppled down next to Lily. They said in unison, "I'm Eunice."

The woman drew near. She looked vaguely familiar to Lily, like someone seen passing in the ship's corridor or sitting across a bar.

"Who's wearing the brooch?" she demanded over the racket of someone outside, banging on the bathroom door. Then Chrissie thrust open the the stall she'd been in. The swinging door cracked Knife Lady in the back. She yelped, plunging forward onto Eunice. She was raising the knife to strike when there was a snap then a sizzle. Knife Lady fell across Eunice's knees. Her limp body rolled onto the linoleum floor.

Eunice and Chrissie stared down at the wilted woman, then over to Lily who held her cane aloft. "Bear's stun gun cane wasn't such a bad gift after all."

The bathroom door broke open as two Alaska state troopers and an Italian hit man piled into the tiny room together.

CHAPTER TEN

Case Notes
May 15, 8 p.m.

I've been tuckered out more frequently on this cruise than any other time in my life. It's as though there's a daily call to arms. I must say I'm getting eager to return to the peace and quiet of Latin's Ranch. The Superstar got underway almost on time. The authorities must now know that neither Hawk Nose nor Rick got back on board. They may think Rick is guilty of murder, but I'd say their eye is more likely on Knife Lady.

At the moment, Eunice and I are wrapped up as tight as reindeer-hot-dogs-in-blankets, out on our balcony loungers. Alejandro provided us with Irish coffees so we are as toasty as we can get while we watch Juneau disappear into the misty channel behind us. After two attempts on Eunice's life, I have to say good riddance to the tough little town. Eunice says she's beginning to question her popularity.

At dinner, Bear brought us up to speed on events at Howlin' Wolf after the cops booted the rest of us out. First, though, I'll write down what I know first hand. I'll start in the ladies room at Howlin' Wolf. Troopers Logan Worth and Lulu Maxwell took control of Knife Lady as she began to recover. Vinny put an arm around Eunice's trembly shoulders and another around mine. It was like having a Roman war god swoop down to protect us. Max took away my stun gun, called for back-up and requested EMTs for Knife Lady. Logan left to corral Dr. Flavenmire. Before they kicked Chrissie out of the

CHAPTER TEN

> bathroom, I whispered to her to tell Bear, Frankie, Charlie and Will we're okay. Rattled but okay.
> The Latin's Ranch gang was still in the L where the ceremony would be taking place if the honoree wasn't trapped in the bathroom. According to Bear, Logan told them to stay put while uniforms ushered everyone else out. Only then did Max allow Vinny to escort Eunice and me in. Fortunately, Max saw fit to give me back my cane first. When Knife Lady recovered from the stun gun blast, she apparently refused help from the EMTs. Max brought her out to the banquet room in handcuffs and joined the rest of us.
> "That's Veronica! She's my girlfriend." Charlie squeaked loud enough for everyone to hear.
> "No she's not. She's my wife."
> When Dr. Flavenmire made that announcement I was thrown for a loop. But things suddenly started to make more sense.
>
>   - Lily Gilbert, Astounded Assistant to PI Bear Jacobs

"She's my girlfriend!" Charlie continued to squeak.

"No she's not." Dr. Flavenmire continued to proclaim.

"No I'm not, you crazy old bastard," Knife Lady hissed at Charlie like an angry goose. Then she rounded on the doctor. "And I'd rather die than be your wife any longer, you miserable bird-brain."

Charlie and Dr. Flavenmire stared at each other and continued to snipe. Both looked pierced through the heart. Meanwhile, Max was reading Veronica her rights as loudly as she could. When finished, she yelled, "Everyone shut the hell up and sit down."

Veronica sat, hands cuffed in front of her, seething and huffing. She kicked out a stilettoed foot, missing Max's ankle by no more than an inch.

"Now then," Max continued, pulling down on her blazer and straightening her scarf as she moved another inch away from her wicked captive. "There's no room for all eleven of you at the station so we're gonna start with you here."

Eleven?

Bear counted. Chrissie, Will, Vinny. Eunice, Lily, Charlie, Frankie, himself. Dr. Flavenmire, Heather and Veronica.

Yep, eleven suspects. Agatha Christie would be proud.

When the rest of the audience had dispersed, Bear had watched them strip the buffet, carrying shrimp away by the handful. He'd also noticed one tall lanky man watching the Latin's Ranch table with bulging brown eyes. When he was herded out by the uniformed cops, he'd even nodded at Bear. The big man was thinking about that until Max cut the thought short.

"Now that the rest are gone, we'll get rid of you as fast as we can, too." Max said. "I mean those of you with no real part in this will be excused."

Logan nodded his agreement. "Let's start with you two." He stared at Will and Chrissie who's arms were intertwined. "Anything to tell us?"

"We only got here yesterday," Chrissie piped up.

"So far, cruising doesn't seem all that fun," Will said.

"Neither of us knows what's going on." Chrissie shrugged.

"You knew enough to smack down Mrs. Flavenmire with a toilet stall door."

"We protect our peeps," Chrissie snapped back at Logan.

"Got it. Okay. You both can leave. We're done with you for now. The officers in the next room will take down your information and statements."

Bear started humming to himself *You'll Never Get Away from Me*. He knew Chrissie wouldn't leave just because some officer of the law told her to. Will might be cool as an embalmer, but Chrissie was hot as a firecracker. A scowl marred her already plain face. "We will do no such thing. We'll stay right here with our charges. We're their aides." She even shook a finger at the officer. "If anything you do causes any of them to collapse, we'll see to it that - "

Lily interrupted. "Chrissie. I'm sure the officers won't mind if you stay."

Dimples appeared in Max's cheeks as she chuckled at the guff her partner was enduring from a mere girl. "Yes, ma'am. We'll handle with care. And you're welcome to stay."

"I'm staying, welcome or not."

"Fine, just fine. See how easy this is?" Max said. "Just a friendly chat. Now you, sir. Who are you and where did you come from?" She looked up, up, up at Vinny.

CHAPTER TEN

"I am Vinny. Vinny Tononi."

"He's our driver," said Bear, having finished humming the chorus. Questioning Vinny was never a good idea.

"Please be quiet, Mr. Jacobs," Logan snapped.

"Ez my aide," said Frankie. "He attend for my wellness."

Logan looked from Bear to Vinny to Frankie. "So you are two more from Latin's Ranch. Two who have not been mentioned to us by Charlie, Lily or Eunice. Or even by PI Bear Jacobs." He stared at them as though they'd been very bad dogs, indeed.

"Or by Deputy Sheriff Josephine Keegan of Washington state, for that matter," added Max.

"Ah! She ez the Cupcake of the Bear!" Frankie said.

Bear tensed. Frankie wasn't used to being questioned, either, and certainly not by a woman. Maybe he'd shoot her. Or Vinny would smash both officers' skulls with brass knuckles. But the old smoothie leaned forward, took Max's hand, kissed it and held on. "I am Francesco Sapienza, at your service. I am at Latin's Ranch with these others. I am old man, and I have my little dove. Otherwise, I would enjoy knowing you more." He cocked his head toward Vinny. "Maybe my associate ... "

"No *padrone*. I am taken." Vinny did his best to look sorry. "Not that you are not a lovely woman, *Signorina* Trooper."

Max turned tomato red under her orange freckles and snatched her hand away.

Logan snickered in unconcealed delight at her discomfort. "Now that it's settled our Max will be going home alone, how do you two fit into all this?"

"I give my little dove the bird."

"You what?" Max and Logan asked in unison.

Bear couldn't really stand to see an investigation go so far awry. So he spoke up once again. "Mr. Sapienza gave Eunice a beautiful - and clearly valuable - brooch in the shape of a bird. An albatross to be exact. To celebrate the award she was to receive here today."

"The bitch paraded around with it just hanging off her boobs. Like a queen bee." Veronica spit the words out like seeds.

Bear continued. "It went missing."

"Night of the murder?" Max asked.

None of the Latin's Ranch gang had ever told the officers that a missing brooch had cut Alita's hand the night she died. They weren't eager to reveal any trail that might lead to Rick. So they launched an immediate offensive to help Bear out of a bind. Even Charlie who, up until then, had been shooting cow eyes at Veronica, tore himself away from his own misery to protect his roomie.

"Maybe, but ..."

"No, I think it was ..."

"I'm sure I had it ... "

"Could have fallen off ..."

They all talked in unison, so nobody heard a thing.

"Nip it!" Logan barked.

Then Bear presented the troopers a peace offering in the form of a half truth. "We wondered if the hawk-nosed man might have stolen it. We realized after the fact that the brooch had gone missing, maybe that night although no one is positive. Maybe it went overboard with him. But we have no way of knowing that. For sure. Of course."

"Very well. We'll leave it for now, okay? But don't think we won't get back to it." Logan sounded weary.

"Alright, Mr. Sapienza and Mr. Tononi. You two may leave and give statements to the officers in the next room," Max said.

"I stay here with my little dove."

"I stay here with my *padrone*."

"Cripes, Max. Can I leave?" Logan groaned.

"You stay here with your partner. But you Latin's Ranchers and your attendants? Get the hell out. I'm not kidding around."

Everyone gathered themselves to go. It looked like a convalescent rodeo by the time chairs, walkers and canes were dispersed. Meanwhile, Eunice muttered, "Hell's bells," and marched over to the podium to pick up what could only be the Arctic Angel Statuette, what with its iceberg of crystal and its golden bird. "I'm not leaving here without this, ceremony be damned."

"Not so fast, PI Bear Jacobs. Sit your ancient chassis back down." Max shot down Chrissie's protest before it could take flight. "We'll get him back to the ship without your help."

"Why keep him here?" Logan asked.

CHAPTER TEN

"Because Deputy Keegan says he's no fool. He can help us. And because he knows more than he's saying."

Bear was delighted to stay although he didn't point it out.

Logan snorted. "We've done a fine job so far, Max. Might as well move on to interview the guilty one. Or ones." He turned toward the fuming female named Veronica. "Your turn to speak up, ma'am."

And speak up she did. Bear had heard angry women in his day. But nothing like this. Her low raspy voice went up, up, up until she shrieked like a fish monger. It wasn't really an interview ... it was more like a tirade.

"I wanted so much out of life. But no. I marry an ornithologist who gets a job in this God forsaken backwater and thinks a woman like me will be happy while he's on icebergs tagging birds."

"Um that's not how ..." Heather made the mistake of interrupting.

"Shut the fuck up, you scrawny excuse for a female."

"Yes, ma'am."

"So here I am, trapped, watching the years go by. I look around. And I see brother Harlan. Better looking, brainier. I ask you. What's a woman to do?"

Her husband cried, "Remember that bit about love and honor, sickness and health?"

"You shut it. I've had it with playing second fiddle to seagulls."

While the cops stared at Veronica, Bear turned his eyes to the doctor and his intern. He saw genuine pain on Flavenmire's face and round-eyed astonishment on Heather's. Both appeared to be hearing Veronica's story for the first time. Bear was willing to bet neither was involved with any kind of PASTA scam. Dr. Flavenmire, who'd been such an obvious suspect, was turning out to be yet another injured party.

Is a red herring on a cruise a red whale?

As an investigator Bear loved it when things were more complex than they seemed. He was enjoying himself and quietly changed his tune to *Happy Days Are Here Again.*

"Harlan kept the books. He knew most of the money was coming in from one particular source. Enough to get the hell out of this dark, wet, fucking excuse of a Dodge. And he wanted me with him. Bye bye, bird man. I ask you, who the hell wouldn't go? Harlan believed he could pull it off, so I did, too."

"I see that," cooed Max. "I understand."

Veronica wasn't buying. "Don't patronize me, curly top. You couldn't possibly know how I felt. We planned it for weeks. Then Harlan blew it. Killed the wrong woman at that senior center down in Washington. I know all blue hairs look alike but still. And then he disappeared from the cruise." She shook her head. "I love him, I guess, but what a moron."

"Were you angry enough at him to kill him?" Max asked.

"Of course I didn't kill him, you nincompoop. He was my ticket out of here. If he's dead, I know it had to be that Eunice bitch. I was so mad I got my neighbor's car and tried running her off the road. But she wasn't in the car. It was those goddamn bastards." She raised her handcuffed hands and wiggled fingers at her targets. "That old man with the beard and the muscle man there. Plus Charlie the Love Boat."

Bear continued to hum.

"You knew Charlie from before the cruise?" Logan asked.

"God no. Met him on the ship to help me keep an eye on the geezer group. Idiot thought I really went for him."

Logan and Max decided to move the rest of the interview to the station. Heather was released, then uniforms took Veronica and Flavenmire away in separate cars. Max told Bear they'd drop him back at the ship.

In the patrol car Bear said, "I know you think this is solved. That Harlan killed Alita and Veronica probably killed Harlan even though she denies it."

"Sounds about right," Max said from the driver's seat.

"But do you know a guy named Eric Blankenship?"

Logan looked over the seatback at Bear. "Blankenship. Yeah. Strange guy and getting stranger. Travel agent without a lot of local business."

"He's a little too close to the cuckoo's nest for the locals. Gets a few out-of-towners." Max pulled up to the dock. "He was at the ceremony today. Why do you ask?"

Bear made a low rumbly noise. "Tall, maybe fifty with a hoody on, bulging brown eyes like a pug's. Longish side burns. Face that smiles in repose. That him?"

"That's him. Sat next to Driver Dan. Probably both came for the free food."

Bear sighed. "Then before I get out, I got something more to tell you."

CHAPTER TEN

✦ ✦ ✦

Jessica brought it on herself. That's what she thought as she cradled Baby Benny who was protesting a nap as though it were a trip to the gallows.

I brought it on myself.

Jessica had offered to babysit because it was her fault that Chrissie was winging her way to the 'north to the future' state. Chrissie's own mother had agreed to keep the toddler, Jacob, but not the four-year-old, Hannah. In fact, Grannie had referred to the child as 'that little hellion.'

Hannah was a handful, Jessica had to admit, cleaning up the spilled juice. Again. Especially when Baby Benny was auditioning for the role of Littlest Monster. The two of them together were a tag team of peskiness.

"Maybe I'm not up to motherhood," she said to Ben with a tired sigh. "Old people are easier. So are horses."

"I think it helps if you work your way into childcare a little more slowly," he said looking up from the Hungry Hungry Hippos game that Hannah was winning. "You know I'm not getting the porch floors stained, right?"

"No matter. The walls aren't getting painted without Chrissie and Will here either. Nothing is getting done while the residents are away. Not like I planned. Except, of course, Aurora's kitchen is sparkling."

Hannah shrieked with delight as she bagged another marble.

"Well, I'm glad this little noise maker is here," Ben said. "It would be awful quiet without the gang."

In fact, everyone at the ranch was missing their old friends. Aurora had cleaned her kitchen to the point of surgical sanitation but had almost nobody to cook for. Her mood had gone from its normal sour to acerbic. Sam thought the poker games with Ben weren't the same without Bear to bluff the hell out of them both.

And it wasn't just the humans that felt the change. Gina Lola, the old workhorse that had belonged to Ben's grandfather, didn't get as many strolls around the paddock now that Ben was up at the house most of the time. Furball missed Charlie's knees to stretch across, and Folly wished Jessica had time for a game of fetch. Furball and Folly were uneasy allies at the best of times, but now they spent the day in the barn to avoid Hannah. The child pulled their ears with glee whenever Jessica didn't dash across the room quite fast enough. For comfort, the orange tabby and black cockadock shared the manger in Gina Lola's stall, although the proximity of the dog made the cat clean its own fur relentlessly.

Jessica watched the game between her husband and the child. She never tired of the easy resolve with which Ben approached any project. His self containment often helped calm her own nerves. But not this time. "Well," she said. "I need to go place an ad for replacement aides. Alita is gone, and it doesn't sound like Rick will be back."

She stood like a person much older than her years and headed off toward her office, baby in her arms. "What can the ad say? Replace two of the finest young people who ever walked the earth? Enjoy a job where everyone will miss your predecessors? Fill a position but never the hole in our hearts?"

Hannah let loose another burst of laughter as her hippo gobbled the last marble.

Ben called after his wife. "The ad can say, become a part of a family who will respect you, appreciate your skills and depend on you to do the best job you can. Who wouldn't want a position like that?"

A knock made Jessica divert her course from her office to the front door. She opened it to a guy big enough and stern enough to be Vinny's twin. In the drive was a caddy limo that had snuck in quieter than a submarine running silent, running deep.

"Ah ... yes?" she said.

"I am from Vinny. Vinny Tononi."

"Ah ... yes?" she repeated, this time noticing the leash that ran from his meaty hands around to the back of his body.

He gave the leash a tug. A furry little face peered around him and up at her. Pointy ears, blue eyes, two tones of gray.

"Is that a husky puppy?" Jessica asked.

"Vinny say thees ez dog from Alaska. To guard for Latin's Ranch. A gift from boss, Frankie Sapienza."

"Ah ... what?" Ben asked, coming up beside his wife. Big Mobster Guy handed the leash to him since Jessica's hands were full of baby.

"Now ez your dog."

They watched the man turn, walk down the stairs, get in the car and drive away.

CHAPTER TEN

"Guard dog?" Ben asked. "From Frankie?"
"That's what the man said."
"Unusual, isn't it? A husky as guard dog?"
"A mobster is an unusual tenant at a family care home."
The puppy, tiring of the human chitchat, entered the house. He saw Folly's dog bed. The one that Furball had appropriated.
"Looks to me like Furball's been evicted," Ben said as the pup lifted a leg and peed on the bed.

✦ ✦ ✦

Bear's face was always fairly haggard, with a roadmap of lines intersecting across his cheeks and puffy pockets under his eyes. But tonight at dinner, Lily thought he was Bear but more so. Deeper lines, puffier pockets. He looked tired. One suspender strap kept slipping, as though his shoulder was weighed down with fatigue.
He was obviously okay, though, because he was enjoying his chow. They all were hungry, having never made it to the Howlin' Wolf buffet.
"Veronica sang like a canary on speed," Bear said. "So pissed at the men in her life, she held back nothing. She may regret it tomorrow but that's not my concern."
"So was Dr. Flavenmire behind it all? Does he want me dead?" Eunice asked as she passed Bear a basket of hot French bread and soft buttery rolls.
"No, Eunice. Comes as a surprise but your Dr. Flavenmire seems to be an innocent in all this. I think he was genuinely stunned that his brother and his wife were in cahoots to steal from your PASTA trust."
"This Flaven person. He ez fool," said Frankie.
"Well, maybe he's just not as observant about people as he is about birds, but I see no reason for you to end your relationship with him, Eunice. He's lost a helluva lot as it is."
During the soup course, Bear explained what else they'd missed after they'd all been sent home from Howlin' Wolf. He told them that the brother, Harlan aka Hawk Nose, was the accountant for PASTA. He and Leland's wife, Veronica, had been having an affair. They intended to pick off

Eunice, take control of the trust, and shut Leland out altogether. "Maybe she was going to kill Harlan, too. But she doesn't seem to have planned that far. She seems to really miss him."

"A *folie à deux*?" asked Lily. "One who convinces the other of something delusional?"

Bear shrugged. "Something like that. Maybe she just believed what she wanted to believe. And Harlan as White Knight fit the bill."

"Guess I was the only one really deluded," Charlie said in a voice an octave lower than usual.

After an embarrassed pause in which everyone looked everywhere except at the dejected old man, Lily started the conversation again. "So Harlan was the Hawk Nosed Man, the one who killed Alita. The one Rick dealt with."

"Yes. And a 'fucking failure just like his ass hat brother' according to Veronica. She was his get-away driver at the senior center when he killed the wrong woman. Hard to forgive a guy a thing like that."

"But she was on the cruise with him anyway?" asked Eunice, just before sipping the Maui onion soup.

Bear nodded. "Seems to have really loved the guy. Also, of course, she wanted to keep an eye on us, to know when they should try again. It was her idea to steal the brooch at the same time, maybe to divert authorities as to the real reason for Eunice's demise. Maybe because she saw no reason not to keep it herself."

Charlie let out a sigh. "Me and my big mouth. I wanted to impress her. Told her about it, that it must be worth a fortune. She knew to watch for it on formal night." Actual tears formed in his eyes. "I am so sorry, Eunice. I'm so sorry I didn't keep my damn yap shut."

"Charlie. It's okay. You didn't know who she was. None of us did."

"Alita might be alive if I didn't - "

"Stop it, Charlie." Bear said, picking up one of the many forks on the table that seemed to have no purpose other than shaking it at Charlie. "Harlan Flavenmire was there to kill Eunice. The brooch had nothing to do with that. It was just an easy theft so he took it. And Alita was in the wrong place at the wrong time. You're not to blame." Bear put the fork back down. Eunice, seated next to him, aligned it again with the rest of the cutlery.

CHAPTER TEN

"I should have known a woman like that wouldn't be interested in a man like me." Charlie slumped like a rag doll losing its stuffing.

Lily felt a shiver of guilt in the pit of her stomach. Charlie's appeal to that woman? It had gnawed at her, too, but she'd ignored it. She'd pushed it away, too busy with more important things to think about. And now Charlie was in pain.

Three of them passed Kleenex and handkerchiefs to Charlie. He sniffed and gulped and blew until he was under control. Meanwhile, main courses of duck l'orange, poached salmon, and peppercorn steak fillets were served with a flourish of sauces and fresh vegetable or pasta side dishes.

"Bear, have Max and Logan called Keegan about that murder at the senior center?" Lily asked.

"It's on their to-do list."

"Veronica doesn't really know what happened to Harlan, right?"

"Well, there's always a chance that the cops still think she killed him. But they're wrong. When Logan told Veronica about the security footage of a man overboard I think she was genuinely surprised." As they ate their meals, Bear explained that Veronica had been furious. She'd felt the need to act. "She got the biggest vehicle she could find and planned to ram it with Eunice in it. But she got Vinny, Charlie and me instead."

Charlie's tears started again. "I told her that, too. That Lily and Eunice were going to go see the town. Thought she might like to join them. God, I'm so worthless. Nothing but a used up old man." He unlocked his wheelchair and left the table, heading out of the dining room.

"I'll go," Will said, standing.

"Just make sure he gets to our room okay, then leave him," Bear said. "Charlie likes time alone when he's feeling this low."

Lily thought about that, how they all knew so much about each other. Charlie's only crime was a little too much trust in his fellow man. Or, in this case, woman.

"You said you thought the driver was actually a woman," Eunice said. "Turns out you were right."

"Seeing how this is hurting Charlie, I'd rather have been wrong."

None of them felt like dessert that evening.

✦ ✦ ✦

Bear and Lily strolled around the Promenade Deck after dinner. Lifeboats hung from riggings above them, looking fragile and small against the background of deep channel water and towering mountains. The wind gusted down through the glaciers of the frozen north, chilling the two old strollers. But the night was clear with no other ships or lights in sight as the *Superstar* negotiated the Lynn Canal on its way to Skagway.

"Lots of ghosts traveling with us here. Sailors and gold miners, lost on their way to the Klondike. Sunken ships are still below us." Lily spoke languidly. She was tired this evening and had opted for the support of her walker in place of the cane. She looked out at the crystalline night and added, "Stars."

"Late at night, on the top deck, you can see into the next light year," Bear replied. "Stars by the millions. Billions."

"Now I know what you do when you can't sleep," she said, smiling up at him. "You count stars." Sleep was not a close friend of the big man. Lily knew he spent many wakeful hours. It was in those hours back home, holding the fractious Baby Benny through the night, that man and boy had bonded so thoroughly. She was glad the stars were around to comfort Bear when Benny wasn't.

They walked for a time in silence, other than the rush of the ocean and her walker wheels punctuated by the *kachunk* of his quad cane on the wooden deck. When she next spoke, Lily patted him on the arm. "You have something to tell me, don't you? I can't take notes if I don't know which ones to sing, you know."

Bear observed her puff of white hair that was a dancing cloud in the wind. "Just hasn't been time without everyone around."

Kachunk. Kachunk.

"Well?" This time she poked him.

"Ouch! I haven't wanted to worry you but maybe I will if you're going to be a brat. Eunice may not be out of the woods yet."

Lily stopped and leaned against a tall wooden chest filled with life vests. "Tell me."

"Jessica called this morning, early. Eunice had received a call from her lawyer. Jess told him where Eunice was and the two of them got to talking. He said a call came in to his office regarding particulars about the Taylor fortune, specifically about Eunice's beneficiaries. The lawyer said he was used to fielding calls especially since Eunice has been known to change her beneficiaries whenever the spirit moves her. Like that incident last Christmas involving the My Fair Pair lingerie store. You remember that."

"Indeed, I do." They moved on again at a meandering pace even slower than before. "What did the lawyer do?"

"Told the caller to get lost. But he thought this particular request was odd because it came from a private party, not a fund or a charity. He wanted Eunice to know about it. He said the guy who called gave him the name of Blankenship. Eric Blankenship."

"Blankenship. Hmmm."

"Yeah. Took me a while, too. Then I remembered Eunice told us that Blankenship was the family name before it became Taylor through marriage."

Lily felt her mind scramble facts together. "You mean someone else might be interested in Eunice's demise? Someone not associated with PASTA? Isn't that a little too coincidental?"

"That's what I thought. So I did some research online this morning before the PASTA debacle. I found an announcement in the Juneau paper regarding the award. Among other things, it listed Eunice as the winner and reported she'd be arriving by cruise ship to accept it."

"So somebody local saw her name. And maybe recognized it."

Bear nodded. "Then I looked up Blankenship. Sure enough, there's an Eric who lives in Juneau."

"A shirttail relative who knew his rich old aunt-twice-removed was coming to town."

"It's a possibility."

"We need to tell Logan and Max."

"I already have. After we finished with Dr. Flavenmire. While they drove me back to the ship. They were going to pay a visit to Eric Blankenship's travel agency after that. Max said they'd call when they knew something."

"Have you heard from them?"

"Nope. I hoped to before we left Juneau. My cell won't work this far from civilization. So we'll have to wait 'til we get to Skagway. If you can come up with a way to keep Eunice on the ship in the morning, do it. Give me time to find out what's going on."

"Eunice, Chrissie and I are getting pedicures on board in the morning. So we don't have a tour booked until after lunch."

"Pedicures. Ugh. Doesn't that tickle?"

"Eunice calls it the price of beauty."

"Cutting your toe nails makes you beautiful?"

"Well, and the polish and creams."

"Women are strange."

"Men aren't?"

"Never denied it. And this one is tired. And cold."

They each had enough energy to finish their stroll in front of their cabin doors.

"Night, Lily."

"Hope you sleep, Bear."

"We've lost Alita and Rick. Couldn't stand to lose Eunice, too."

"No."

"Rick's out there, Lily. Alone and scared, maybe in the cold and dark. He hasn't even had time to grieve for his girl. And now you can bet the cops will look at him for the disappearance of Harlan Flavenmire and Alita as well. Some things are just too damn hard."

"The whole thing sucks. But without you, he would never have gotten to any kind of freedom. Don't sink too deep in the depths, Bear. The rest of us need your help."

He nodded. "I'll sleep well when we're all back home."

CHAPTER ELEVEN

Case Notes
May 16, 9 p.m.

I should have the bandage off tomorrow about the time my black eye gets as colorful as the Northern Lights. But no more pain killers. The one I took late this morning made me loopier than ever. Bear, nasty man that he is, asked how I could tell.

Anyhoo, let me start at bedtime last night. That's when I told Eunice about the lawyer's call from Eric Blankenship and Bear's follow-up research. She's never met the Eric guy or any other Blankenship, for that matter. She says it wouldn't surprise her, though, since she seems to be on a lot of shit lists.

First thing this morning, Eunice, Chrissie and I were prisoners in overgrown leather chairs with attached jetted baths that whirled and pummeled our feet. Then our toenails were buffed, filed, polished and placed in yellow foam separators to dry. Eunice's digits are now a deep red called The Beet Goes On. Chrissie is Central Park After Dark, sort of a deep purple. Me? I'm Naughty Nude Nightie. While we dried, Chrissie and Eunice couldn't move their feet. I couldn't move my foot. That's okay because we weren't going anywhere ... a trio of operators attacked our fingernails.

I told Eunice that Bear asked me to keep her aboard this morning until he had a chance to consult Max and Logan. Being held hostage in the salon made that easy to do. Like Eunice said, "As if I'd stay

BEAR AT SEA

put if I didn't want to. But have you seen it out there? Snow. In May. I'm not that eager to see the sites of Skagway."

Chrissie didn't agree. She's mega-excited since this is her first trip out of Washington State. "Will and I are taking the White Pass Railway this afternoon. Narrow gage ... rickety trestles over deep ravines ... Torment Valley. Following the seekers of gold."

Eunice harrumphed. "At least your nails will be lovely when they find your body under a fresh avalanche."

"Now Miss Eunice. Where's your sense of adventure? Bet you've never panned for gold."

"I've have enough adventure for one trip. And someone else is panning for my gold."

I've read enough tour lit to know Skagway was the gateway to the gold fields in the very late 1800s. After the rush the town faded to oblivion. Now the saloons, dance halls and gambling houses host tourists. Excursions are for younger limbs than ours ... zip lines, rock climbing, rafting. I'm damn glad to be indoors for the day.

"Besides, local entertainers are coming on board this afternoon," Eunice said, "to tell the Skagway story in the Superstar Oscar *theatre. Lots of banjos, I imagine."*

"Sounds good. Maybe I'll stay with you," Chrissie said, her sense of duty at conflict with her sense of adventure.

"Don't be silly. You and Will take a break. Have fun." Eunice made a motion like shooing chickens, much to the nail technician's annoyance. Chrissie finally agreed to leave us onboard, safe and sound and warm. What could go wrong before noon on a cruise ship?

Excuse me while I put an ice pack on my forehead and close my other eye, too.

    - Lily Gilbert So-I-Was-Wrong Assistant to PI Bear Jacobs

---

In paper scuffs from the spa, Eunice and Lily waddled like ducks with their toe separators still in place. Better to chance a fall than mess up a polish job before it was dry.

They elevatored from the top deck to their cabin level. The gilt-infested

CHAPTER ELEVEN

lift was usually empty on a port day. But after they shuffled in and took a position at the back, the ship's cruise director crammed in with a group of travel agents.

"Sorry ladies," he said. "Just showing these folks the ship."

"Watch the tootsies, watch the tootsies," Eunice yelped.

Seeing several agents turn to stare, Lily added, "She doesn't mean *we're* tootsies. She means our toes. They're tootsies."

A good hearted chuckle erupted into a Q&A session with the agents questioning the salon, the spa and other ship board amenities. The two old friends gave the *Superstar* enthusiastic thumbs up to the clear delight of the cruise director.

"After all, it's not the ship's fault that everyone wants to ice me." When the elevator door whooshed open on their floor, the startled agents parted as smoothly as the Red Sea to allow Lily and Eunice out. Eunice continued in the hard-boiled lingo she loved. "Poison me with lead, close my yap, zap my button with Chicago lightning."

Lily said, "You wouldn't think Skagway would have so many travel agents."

Eunice replied, "Dose me with Nevada gas," as they minced on down the corridor. Lily knew the routine would stop sooner or later but only if she didn't complain.

Alejandro, who had seen his ladies exit the elevator and was now escorting them, looked a question at Eunice but answered Lily. "No, they probably don't have many agents. But since we're such a big deal in the tourist business, they come from all over the state for these ship tours. Helps them sound like experts to have seen the ships they're recommending."

"Jab my beezer with the roscoe," Eunice said as Alejandro opened their cabin door and helped them place a room service luncheon for delivery to the suite in an hour. After setting their table he left, but Lily heard him knock right away. She opened the door to see what he needed.

A tall lanky man with brown bulging eyes shoved her against the wall, pushing his way into the room. He passed without seeing her at all, drawing a bead on Eunice. Lily yelled, "Hey!" and only then did he look at her.

In that brief second, Lily saw madness.

Then he turned back to Eunice. "Hello, Auntie," he said. Lily knew instantly this was Eric Blankenship. She had seen him before, but not at the Howlin' Wolf where Bear had picked him out. In the group of travel agents. On the elevator. He'd been one of them.

"Auntie?" Eunice said, sitting on the edge of a dining chair. She cocked her head. It looked like the weight of the dangly earring on that side might pull her over.

Where is Bear?

Lily thought he must be with Max and Logan. That had been his plan for the morning. But were they still in town or on the ship?

And Vinny? Mr. Weaponry?

"Don't you recognize me, Aunt Eunice?" the man said. In repose, his face seemed to smile.

"I do, young man," said Lily. "You're Eric Blankenship. You know, Eunice. The Blankenships on your husband's side. He's the boy you've been looking for."

Eric turned to Lily. She saw confusion followed by a hint of delight as if he was pleased to be recognized.

"Exactly!" he said, before turning back to Eunice. "Your hired help has spilled the beans. So you've been looking for me! And I've been looking for you!"

"Ah, yes. Yes, that's true. How are you, my boy?"

Bless Eunice for playing along. And dropping the hard-boiled bullshit.

"You've been looking for your heir for so long now," Lily said moving closer to Eunice, trying to get between her friend and this man.

The madness in Eric howled, "GET AWAY FROM HER." Lily stepped back and the smile returned to his face. "And I found you before you found me. How fun!"

Lily knew Eunice would follow her lead. If only they could ...

Eric picked up a steak knife from the table that Alejandro had set. He frowned. "The problem is, Aunt Eunice, I need the money now. Business is poor so I am, too."

"But Eric, I don't ..."

"DON'T TELL ME DON'T. DON'T ANYTHING. THE MONEY WAS NEVER YOURS, YOU THIEF." He snarled then swallowed the anger. "Excuse me, that was ruder than necessary."

CHAPTER ELEVEN

Folie à Un.

Delusion of one.

Concentrate.

Lily had to do something. "But Eric, your Aunt Eunice can't give the money to you."

He rounded on her. "She can't?"

Eunice echoed, "I can't?"

"No. You see, Eunice is ... married. And her husband inherits everything now if she dies."

"What the fuck? Married to who? What have you done, Aunt Eunice?" The man spun from one old woman to the other.

"The man's name is Alvin Jacobs. He gets the money if Eunice dies."

"Oh yes. My Bear. My beloved," cooed Eunice. "He inherits. Yes, indeed."

A wave of fury engulfed Eric. "You mean that fat old bastard at Howlin' Wolf? Where the fuck is he now?"

"I'm sure he'd want you to have your just reward. All you have to do is ask, right, Eunice?"

"Of course. We both know the money should be yours. That's why I was trying to find you, my dear boy."

"Let's call him now." Lily pulled her phone from her sweater pocket and punched the single button that would connect her to Bear.

Eric batted the phone away. It bounced onto the floor at Lily's feet.

Eunice stepped forward and took his arm. "I'm sure Bear will be in his cabin. With Max and Logan. We can take you."

"Okay. You, Aunt Eunice. But not you. You're not part of this." He reached out and slapped the side of Lily's head. She wobbled, grabbed the back of a chair and lowered herself onto the seat as her ear rang. With only one leg, her balance was already compromised. When Blankenship slapped her again, she yelped and crumpled onto the floor. Far away, she heard Eunice scream her name, then everything lost focus.

Bear's phone rang, and it took a while to ferret it out of the right pocket. When he answered it, he heard Lily talking to someone else, saying she was sure Bear was in his cabin. Then he heard Eunice's voice and a man answer. She said they were coming to find him. The man yelled loud enough for Bear to hear the words, "You're not part of this."

Next Bear heard a slap, a yelp and a thud. "Lily?" he whispered. "Lily?" No answer.

He turned to Max and Logan. "Get to Eunice now."

As the cops leapt for his cabin door, Bear punched in the digit for Vinny. "Help. Come by the east elevator. Down the corridor. Fast."

He *kachunked* behind the two cops as they raced out of the room. Then they hit the brakes. Eunice and Blankenship were not far down the hall. He held a knife at her throat and had her arm in his grasp.

"Put the --"

Bear cut off Logan's order and pushed past him.

"Hi, Eunice," the big man said calmly through a big smile. "Hey there. What you got on your feet?"

It was such an unexpected comment that Eric pulled her to a stop and looked down.

Eunice passed information to Bear. "Hello, my dear husband. Just toe separators. Make me go even slower. Like a duck. Ha, ha."

Bear caught on. "Well, wife of mine, you are always worth waiting for."

"Bear, this young man is my nephew, Eric. Your nephew, too, now that we are married. He's the one I've been looking for. Now we can sign the fortune over to him, right where it belongs."

"Eric! Good to meet you, son." Bear moved forward with a jovial grin and held out a hand. "Put 'er there." He looked into the deranged face, and he understood. This was not an evil man but a lost one. Nonetheless, the outcome to Eunice could be the same.

"No. Get back. You're confusing me. All of you. Get back." Eric held tighter to Eunice's chicken bone arm.

Bear prayed the two cops would stay frozen in position behind him.

CHAPTER ELEVEN

"Easy, son. We just want to get you the money so you can leave and nobody gets hurt."

"It's mine."

"Yes it is," Bear agreed.

The cops held their stance. Bear held his, a hand still out toward Blankenship. Then the mental demons took control and Eric shrieked, "YOU'RE FUCKING WITH ME. I'LL KILL THE BITCH AND YOU WON'T -"

Vinny hit him from behind as fast and lethal as a killer whale.

Eunice collapsed against the wall, her mouth open but the scream stuck inside. Eric, with Vinny on top, slid to a stop at the cops' feet.

Max and Logan remained still for a split second, dazed, then reached down together to capture the villain buried under the hit man.

Only Bear was already underway, roaring for the steward to open the door and moving at painful speed toward Lily.

✦ ✦ ✦

Voices and thrashing at the cabin entrance irritated Lily from her stupor into consciousness. "Shut up," she snapped or at least that's what she thought she said. Later, Bear clarified that she'd said, "Shut the hell up."

Alejandro was first through the door, calling the ship's doctor as Lily tried to lift herself off the floor. But the cabin began to rock.

Are we at sea? Is there a storm?

She sat back down on the floor as Bear, breathing heavily, pushed through the door next. He sat in the dining chair she clung to, and she leaned against him. She let him cradle her head in his massive paws, holding her as still as he could.

"I'm okay, Bear," Lily muttered. "I'll be fine when the cabin stops whirling." Meanwhile, Eunice appeared and, like an angel, placed a cool cloth on Lily's head.

Bear held on until medics appeared with a gurney, lifted Lily away from him and whisked her off to the ship's infirmary. She was, of course, protesting in a Lily-like fashion. "I can't leave now. Who'll keep the case notes?"

Bear started to stand, but Eunice stopped him. "You were here for her, Bear. Now she's more likely to want me. A lady friend." She leaned down and kissed his old cheek. "The cops have taken Eric off the ship but said they'd be back to talk with us before we leave port."

Alejandro, Eunice and the medical team left. The cabin, after the flurry and commotion, was abruptly silent. Bear sat still for a long time. Then, in a release of dread, he cried.

✦ ✦ ✦

By late afternoon, things had gone from a high boil to a gentle simmer in the lives of the Latin's Ranch group. Bear had gathered everyone around Lily and Eunice in their suite to await Max and Logan. Only Chrissie and Will, under protest, were missing. Eunice had sent them to buy a few supplies before the ship left port at six o'clock, heading for Kodiak.

Lily was lying on the sofa under a soft blanket, looking fragile but alert. If Bear had to guess, she was woozy with painkillers. The swelling and bruising distorting her face incensed him each time he looked at her. Nonetheless, he had calmed himself since the crazy morning events. Now that he could see Lily was battered but not beaten, he could give a little thought to his own pain. His legs throbbed from his gallop down the corridor, and he knew he'd pay for that extreme sport with a sleepless night.

Charlie sat in his wheelchair talking about Kodiak as he flipped through his book on Alaska. It would be their next port of call after a day at sea. "Fishing seems to be the only good way to make a living there these days." He looked up and added, "And if you've seen those TV shows about fishing in these waters, sounds like a good way to die, too."

"Surely there's something more pleasant in that book to talk about than dying," said Eunice.

"I don't know. Tsunamis are a big risk. Earthquakes even bigger. For sure Kodiak bears. Any of them related to you, Bear?"

"I meant something we could go see, Charlie. You know, tourist things."

CHAPTER ELEVEN

"Well ... lots of Alutiiq natives. Like Rick. Maybe we'll see him."

"No we won't, Charlie. And if you ever do, wheel yourself away. Don't point him out or call his name." Bear wasn't really worried about it. He knew they'd never see the boy again, assuming he'd even made it to Kodiak.

"Oh." Charlie showed the good sense to drop the subject. "Well, there's a Russian Orthodox church built back in the fur trader days. A Russian museum, too."

Frankie sat close to Eunice, trembling slightly. He usually stayed in his room when his Parkinson's became visible. Bear understood Frankie's reluctance to appear weak in public; dons never displayed vulnerability. But the old man's little dove might need him now, so at her side he sat.

We all sit at each other's side when the chips are down.

Bear never really felt a part of a group before, not like this. He treasured the feeling. Latin's Ranch had done more than save his rotten old hide. It gave him purpose.

Only Vinny stood outside the circle, near the door of the cabin. On alert. Always on alert. When the knock on the door came, the one they had been waiting for, he was there to answer it.

The two state troopers came into the room and were greeted with a mixed bag of pleasure and unease. As likable as these two were, they were still cops. Bear felt the group's anxiety float through the air. "Thanks for coming back, Max. Logan. Bring us up to date." He tried to make it sound like this was no more than a social call.

Logan lowered his long, rawboned frame into a delicate chair, nearly overpowering it. "Bring you up to date? Actually, if I had my way we'd arrest the batch of you for obstruction of justice. But Max here says the jail is plumb out of geriatric facilities for codgers, especially those with an armory in their mobility equipment." Logan smiled for a moment although Bear doubted its sincerity. "So we're hoping you can answer a question for us, not the other way around."

Max, only two-thirds Logan's height, had settled easily into a matching chair next to Lily. As if ignoring her partner, she asked, "How are you doing, Mrs. Gilbert?"

Lily gave her a thumbs up and a watered down smile. She pulled the blanket a little closer to her chin.

"That black eye will give you quite a story to tell to passengers on your way back home," Max the Peacemaker said.

I like this lady cop.

Bear wondered why women often seemed more likeable to him. More reasonable. He'd have to think about that when there was time. Right now there was already plenty on his mind. "I haven't brought everyone up to speed on why you were here this morning, Max."

"Yeah," Charlie said. "When did you get to Skagway? Didn't expect you here."

"We flew in on a state plane first thing this morning. Just a short hop from Juneau. Got here before your ship did."

"Why?"

"Yesterday when we went to Blankenship's office, he was gone. Wasn't at his apartment, either. We worried about that."

Logan crossed one long leg over the other. "We didn't think he'd gotten on the ship in Juneau before it left. If he was making a go at Eunice, it had to be here."

"We thought we might apprehend him on the dock waiting for your ship to come in, so to speak. But he wasn't there. After the morning excursions left, we came aboard and met up with Bear."

"Blankenship claims he arrived much later, getting aboard as part of an official tour for travel agents. He had the credentials for that."

"Where is he now?" Eunice asked.

"At the Skagway station. But we'll take him in the police plane back to Juneau with us when we leave."

"Has he been charged? What will become of him?" Eunice asked. Bear stared at her. Were her features beginning to look all sad and mushy? Was Eunice giving in to her heart instead of her head?

"Not charged. Yet. But attempted murder comes to mind as a start. And we'll have to be sure he has no connection to the Flavenmire fiasco."

Eunice sighed. "Yes, I suppose Eric did intend to kill me. And he wasn't the first in that line. Maybe I'm just getting used to it. But, officers, I'd like you to keep in mind that Eric Blankenship seemed genuinely deranged. And he is family, even if it is a distant connection. I'd request you go easy on him."

CHAPTER ELEVEN

Frankie flinched. "I request you hang him by his -"

"Eunice has a point, officers," Lily said weakly. It was enough to stop Frankie's ire. "He seemed more deluded than evil to me, too."

"Well, we'll see how the questioning goes," Max said. "No need to make that decision yet. A mental health assessment will be done in Juneau."

"When you going back?"

"Soon as we leave here. Which we should be doing." Logan unwound himself and stood. "If anything more is needed from you, you'll be met in Kodiak. Other cases are claiming the two of us now. We'll send all our notes to Detective Keegan in case she needs them. But nobody from the feds, the state or the cruise line are pushing for more. And I take it you don't feel the need for the investigation going any deeper."

Bear had to laugh as everyone shook their heads in unison. "No, you're right. I think we all just want to put this behind us."

"Course there's that one remaining mystery that keeps tickling at us," Logan said, scratching his chin. Max peered directly at Bear who suddenly felt like a beetle on a pin.

"Remaining mystery?"

"Yeah. About the aide, Rick Peters." Max stood up next to Logan, but never broke eye contact with Bear. "Rick Peters and Alita Aarons were seen together by dozens of passengers on the ship. Quite, ah, demonstrative. One guest suggested they were the best show on board the whole trip."

"Really?" Bear tried to appear guileless but he was crappy at it.

"Yet none of you mentioned that the two were in a relationship."

"They were?' Charlie turned to the group. "Did you know that? I didn't know that."

Bear held up a hand. "It's okay, Charlie. I'll admit, we guessed at it. We had a pool on when they would marry."

"Ah. So the young man loved the young woman. The fairy tale," Max said as she closed her notebook and put it into her shoulder bag.

"Would you say he might have murdered the person who murdered her?" Logan seemed to be considering his cuticles.

"You ready to pounce, officers?" Bear said.

"No. We're off the case now. On to others."

"Well then. Maybe he would have. Wouldn't you in his shoes?"

"Commit murder?" Max asked. "No. I'm employed to uphold laws, not break them. If I learn more, I will act on it."

Bear heard the warning. "Then our guess is the young man changed his mind. He got cold feet. Couldn't face telling Alita that the relationship was over, so he jumped ship. Wouldn't be the first guy to run from the altar."

"Then that will have to do. But his name is on the books now. We'll be keeping an ear and eye open. Can't say what the tribes might do. In case he decides to explore his heritage and all."

✦ ✦ ✦

Chrissie and Will made it back from their shopping trip just after the troopers left. A briskness of youth accompanied them, like a whoosh of fresh air. Their good humor painted the room.

"What have you two been up to?" Lily asked. Her voice sounded stronger even to herself. Maybe the last of the meds was wearing off.

"It was Eunice's idea," Chrissie said, "that we hunt down a concealer for you. And dark glasses."

As Chrissie pulled a wide framed, sparkling bowed pair of dark glasses from a bag, Eunice spoke up. "I know you want to look your best for the rest of the cruise. And you don't want people staring as your skin turns Technicolor."

Lily didn't say what she was thinking. If you were going to send anybody for fashion items and make-up it would have been Alita. Not Chrissie.

Chrissie did say what she was thinking. "Of course, Alita would have been better at this than I am. I have no knowledge of balms and ointments and lotions and magic."

"Oh, my dear, you perform magic all the time. Without your care, I would never had recovered enough to try a prosthesis."

As Chrissie beamed with the compliment, Will said, "She was so worried. Then I reminded her of what I can do with a concealer and a couple color sticks." He began to pull tiny tubs and tubes and sponges out of a Sizzlin' Skagway shopping bag. "No one outshines an embalmer in the

CHAPTER ELEVEN

make-up department."

"Oh!" cried Eunice but Will continued. "I got just what you'll need. Several things really, because you'll change color as the bruise gets older. I suggest a green base for red bruising, but you need white for brown, and of course, lavender for yellow."

"Oh!" cried Eunice again, clearly distressed as her hands fluttered in front of her. "I didn't think ... Lily, I didn't mean you look like death or anything. I ..."

"C'mon Will," Lily said. "Show me what you can do with *Death's Door* and *Look Alive!*"

"Got any *Mask My Mistakes*? I could use a shitload of that," said Charlie.

✦ ✦ ✦

Jo Keegan stopped by Latin's Ranch to spend a few minutes with Jessica. It turned into dinner with Jessica, Ben, Hannah and Sam. Aurora, thrilled to have another mouth to fill with her *carne asada de grupa*, wouldn't let the deputy leave until she was so full she might never fit in her cruiser again.

"Your new partner, you like him? He is a better man than the last one?" Aurora had never recovered from the last partner, Detective Hot Stuff. Either from his killer looks or his perfidy.

Keegan paused, cocked her head and gave some thought to Brandon Orwell. Then she said, "Yes. I like my new partner. He's a good kid. And he'll learn. For sure, he is a better man than the last one."

Through dinner, she told them about the call from Alaska trooper Lulu Maxwell. It sounded to her like the Latin's Ranch party was finally in for some days of smooth sailing.

"So they are out of danger?" Jessica asked.

"Well, at least from the Flavenmires and Blankenships. Who knows what will happen if one of them wins another award next week?"

While Ben poured all the adults another glass of wine, all hell broke loose in the kitchen.

"OUT! GET OUT!" Aurora screamed. "BAD! BAD!"

Keegan jumped. "Is she all right?"

"Oh yes, that's just the pack cutting through her domain."

A fat cat tore from the kitchen through the dining room into the living room where the canaries set up a melodic shout of their own. Shortly behind the cat came Folly, doing his best on his short doxy legs. Next in line was a big, gamboling puppy with a cookie in its mouth. Finally, Aurora appeared with a tray in her hands and slapped it down on the table. "One less ameretti with the fruit cups, I am afraid. This puppy, he is a *gamberro*."

Keegan was fairly sure a gamberro was nothing good. But those damn almond macaroons were. She'd had them before and figured she'd eat all there were on that tray. Good thing the pup had made off with a share of them.

"New dog, huh?"

"Yes. A gift from Frankie," Jessica answered. "He appears to believe we need a guard dog, so while they were in Ketchikan, he sent Vinny to get a brooch for Eunice and a puppy for us."

"So far we need something to guard us from the dog," Sam pointed out.

Ben nodded. "He's chewed all our magazines and the coffee table legs and claimed every baseboard as his territory."

"I leave no shoes or underwear on the floor anymore," Jessica added.

"Think I'll hitch him up to Sitting Bull since we don't have a dog sled. Maybe pulling a cart would slow him down." Sam rarely said so many words aloud in a row.

"The only one around here who can control him is Folly. The pup listens to him for whatever reason," Jessica said.

"And Gina Lola," Sam added. "She showed him how big a horse's teeth are just in case they're needed."

"What's his name?" Keegan asked.

"Well, with Folly around, I think he should be Seward, don't you?"

"No. He's a Klondike, for sure."

"Gold Rush."

"Big Foot. Just look at those paws."

"Ice King."

"Borealis."

CHAPTER ELEVEN

"Old Blue Eyes."
"Bad Ass."
"Paper Chase."
"Gamberro."

The later it got, the worse the names. Jessica wrote each suggestion down on a strip of paper and put them all in a clean wine glass. Sam Hart drew the winning name. He snickered.

"Looks like our newest resident is Good Fella."

CHAPTER TWELVE

Case Notes
May 18, 5 p.m.

The next day was another at sea as the Superstar *sailed into the Gulf of Alaska, along the coast. We passed by Homer and sailed through the night to Kodiak, arriving this morning.*
Yesterday was long in terms of the daylight hours in the Land of the Midnight Sun. Stretches of this coastline, known as The Roof of North America - *since Alaska just seems to attract nicknames - are as magnificent as anywhere on earth. Vast glaciers, unexplored mountains, ice bergs, orca pods and humpbacks.*
It was a day of much needed rest for us. We all felt the aftereffects of too much exertion, each in our own way. True to his word, Will fixed me up with a layer of make-up thick as grout. It hid the worst of the bruising and the dark glasses did the rest, covering half my face like glittery goggles. I looked like a dressy bug.
Eunice and I relaxed on the warm deck with the covered pool and watched this magnificent world float by. Later we ventured into the casino and I taught her the basics of Blackjack. It's been a lot of years since I've played but it all came back to me. I was a dealer in Vegas for a while when ... but that's another story.
Chrissie and Will did as many of the ship activities as they possibly could. They took a make-the-perfect-martini class, toured the ship's galley, learned how to carve melons into mermaids. Bear and Frank-

CHAPTER TWELVE

ie enjoyed bullshitting each other at chess all afternoon, so Vinny got a little time off for a massage in the spa. Charlie, who seems to be living proof that old dogs can't learn new tricks, has met another woman. At least this one is more than half his age. And he's back to his sunnier self.

Last night we dressed in formal duds again for the final time on the cruise. After dinner, we went to a bar and watched Chrissie and Will challenge other couples at karaoke. I thought they might not be very good. But I was wrong. They were absolutely dreadful.

This morning when we sailed into Kodiak, Eunice and I were both ready for a little activity after our lazy day aboard. We wanted to stretch our legs, or leg as the case may be. We'd disembarked and started walking in the watery sun when a woman came dashing toward us.

"Not another one!" yelled Eunice, raising her sequined tote bag to take a swing.

"Wait!" I replied, grabbing her arm. I realized the designer-parkaed, leather-booted woman looked familiar. Sure enough. She pushed back the hood. It was Sylvia.

Don't ever let it be said that my daughter is predictable. Used to be. Not anymore.

Our walk quickly morphed into coffee in a diner on the waterfront. It seems my daughter got worried about me. Not because of what I said, but because of what I hadn't been saying. Not enough texts and phone calls. I thought about getting mad. My daughter shouldn't be checking up on me. But of course, there I was with a black eye since I'd told Will I wanted a day off from looking like a drag queen. So it would have been hard to argue.

The whole story tumbled out, Eunice and I sharing the explanation. Sylvia said she had threatened the cruise line to let her come on board and go home with us. She played the you-have-allowed-their-aides-to-die-and-placed-them-in-extreme-danger card. They said she could stay in our suite but she booked an empty cabin just down the hall. "Not to interfere with your privacy," she said.

Maybe. But I'm thinking she's hoping we don't interfere with her privacy as she does a little interfering with Vinny's in the privacy of that cabin. Not that I would ever say such a thing.

Syl went on her way to get through the boarding process and no doubt, hunt down the hunk, but Eunice and I decided to explore the Russian museum in Kodiak. It was the most famous in the state for relics from the fur trading era, but at that it was still small. No bigger than a frontier home which, once upon a time, it had been. We were early so they had just opened. A cheery woman with a Swiffer was dusting glass display cabinets and counter tops as we slowly moved from exhibit to exhibit.

Suddenly I heard Eunice draw in her breath. She'd come to a standstill just ahead of me. In fact, I bumped into her.

"When did you get this?" Eunice said to the room at large."Where did you get it?"

The woman with the Swiffer answered. "Isn't it lovely? It was donated just days ago, and we put it on view right away. A thing of legend. If you're from the cruise ship you're among the first tourists to see it. But I'm sure it will be a favorite from now on."

When I saw it, I was as dumbfounded as Eunice. "Who brought it in?"

"A young Indian man, um, I mean Native American. I thought he was donating for the local tribe. But no. At least it isn't a native name or even a native item. We haven't done all the research yet."

As we stared at the jeweled egg, open to reveal the beautiful white and gold bird inside, the Swiffer Woman continued. "He gave us the name of the donor. That's all we have for the display card so far."

Eunice and I bent down to look at the card. Sure enough. It read: Donated by Alita Aarons.

We took a cab back to the ship, maybe the only such vehicle in Kodiak. Neither of us spoke. I doubt either of us could without tears washing our words away. What a powerful brew sorrow and joy make when mixed together. Rick had made it to Kodiak. He had made it home.

We sat on our balcony and stared out at the water and islands and mountains. Somewhere he was there. But our amazement wasn't yet done.

A ruffle of feathers caught our attention. It was a bird. White with a

CHAPTER TWELVE

blue tipped pink beak doing fly-bys just off our balcony.

"Oh," breathed Eunice in a whisper worthy of a cathedral. "I've never seen one before in all these years of loving them. The short-tailed albatross. So rare. So beautiful."

It flew in great arcs, swooping around again and again as though fascinated by the big white ship, as much a sea creature as the bird. After giving our eyes a lasting impression of its graceful shape, enormous wing span and perfectly adequate tail, the bird finally flew on its way. We watched it until it disappeared on its long flight to somewhere.

"I believe Alita has come home, too," Eunice said.

I believe my old friend is right.

- Lily Gilbert, Enchanted Assistant to PI Bear Jacobs

THE END

Author's Acknowledgments

For insight on cruising, I am indebted to personal experience with several cruise lines and trips to Alaska, as well as to my sister and travel partner, Donna Whichello. For additional factual content in *Bear at Sea*, I thank many experts, librarians and websites.

I am sincerely grateful to Heidi Hansen, Jon Eekhoff, Melee Vander Veldt, Beth Pratt and Kimberly Minard, all members of my excellent critique group. To the readers of the earlier Bear books, you are my cheerleaders when I am flagging. Special thanks to Monique Evans Johnson for saving me from typos, word-os, and the occasional weird sentence.

I am indebted to Bear, Lily, Eunice, Charlie and the rest of the Latin's Ranch gang who have been an inspiration to me since they first appeared in *Fun House Chronicles*. That was the story of how they got together ... the Bear Jacobs Mystery series is the story of their friendship in the days that follow.

About the Author

Linda B. Myers won her first creative contest in the sixth grade for her *Clean Up Fix Up Paint Up* poster. After a Chicago marketing career, she traded in her snow boots for rain boots and moved to the Pacific Northwest with her Maltese Dotty. You can visit with Linda on her blog at www.lindabmyers.com

The Bear Jacobs Mystery Series

Available on www.amazon.com

Meet retired PI Bear Jacobs, his eWatson Lily Gilbert, and the rest of the quirky residents at Latin's Ranch Adult Family Home in the Pacific Northwest. Yes, they are infirm. Yes, they gripe. But all the while, they solve crimes, dodge bullets and stand tall on their canes, walkers and wheels. Enjoy this whole series of cozies with bite.

Book One. **Bear in Mind**

The Latin's Ranch residents investigate the case of Charlie's missing wife. Is she a heart breaking bitch who abandoned her hubby? Or is a madman attacking older women? When others in the community disappear, Bear and his gang follow a dangerous and twisted trail to a surprising conclusion.

Book Two. **Hard to Bear**

A vicious crew is producing old-fashioned snuff films with a violent new twist: custom-order murder for sale. The Latin's Ranch gang takes on the villains behind this updated evil, coming under danger themselves. Bear joins forces with an avenging mob family, a special forces soldier tormented by PTSD, and a pack of mad dogs on the loose in the Pacific Northwest woods.

Novella One. **Bear Claus**

PI Bear Jacobs is mired down with seasonal depression until his e-Watson, Lily, finds him a mystery to solve. The trail is both fun and fearsome as it leads from theft in the My Fair Pair lingerie shop through a local casino to a dangerous solution in the Northwest Forest. Bear Claus is a Christmas novella.

Book Three. **Bear at Sea**

When Eunice wins the Arctic Angel Award, the Latin's Ranch gang cruises to Alaska to pick up her prize. But high life on shipboard is dashed by low life murderers and thieves. One of their aides is struck down, and Eunice's life is threatened not once but twice. The gang takes action, endangering themselves to solve the case of the short-tailed albatross.

Check Out Linda's Other Novels:

Fun House Chronicles

Self-reliant Lily Gilbert enters a nursing home ready to kick administrative butt until the chill realities of the place nearly flatten her. She calls it the Fun House for the scary sights and sounds that await her there. Soon other quirky residents and caregivers draw Lily and her daughter in as they grapple with their own challenges. Lily discovers each stage of life can be its own adventure with more than a few surprises along the way. The characters in the Bear Jacob Mystery series made their first appearance in *Fun House Chronicles*.

Lessons of Evil

Oregon, 1989. Psychologist Laura Covington joins a community mental health department. One of her new clients is so traumatized he suffers Multiple Personality Disorder. Through him, Laura discovers a desert cult and the vicious psychopath who commands it. Laura has unleashed dangerous secrets and now, she must decide how far she is willing to go to protect everything she loves. This is psychological suspense geared to keep you guessing as it builds toward its unpredictable conclusion.

A Time of Secrets: A Big Island Mystery

Life is uncomplicated in a Big Island village until Maile Palea, an 8-year-old girl, disappears. Twelve years later she is still missing. This is the story of her sister and brother who never give up trying to find her and cannot heal until they do, of a village that no longer feels safe from a changing world, and of a perpetrator who discovers what disastrous things happen when you keep secrets too long. A perfect read for fans of edgy suspense and hot Hawaiian nights.

The Slightly Altered History of Cascadia

First Female and Old Man Above have screwed up in the creation of humans and call on the spirit Cascadia to fix it. With the help of her human familiar, a magic blade, a flying bear and a logging horse named Blue, Cascadia takes on a killer, ends the traffic in bear gall bladders, and leads a war against a survivalist group intent on slavery. She devises a plan for a better kind of human. Will the gods agree or scrap the whole damn planet? This satirical adult fantasy is a fast-paced quest through history, mythology and modern day ills.

Excerpt from

A Time of Secrets

By Linda B. Myers

If you like edgy suspense and hot tropical nights, this Big Island Mystery is for you.

Excerpt from A TIME OF SECRETS

PREFACE

I wasn't always *lolo*, you know. People didn't think I was crazy. Keeping silent is where I went so wrong. And nothing was ever right again.

- My Book of Revelation
Excerpt from the Year 2012

CHAPTER ONE

Tattooist Found Guilty
of 'Ass-inine' Crime

By Jackson O'Reilly

Excerpt from the *Keawalani Voice,* 2012

    Kaleo Palea, proprietor of the Tat Joint, has been sentenced to thirty days in the Hamakua District jail. The judge also closed his tattoo shop for six months, a little extra punishment to dissuade him from vandalizing the backsides of others in the future.
    In the opinion of most villagers, including this reporter, Kaleo Palea does not deserve his fate. "He's not a bad guy," his sister Nani Palea said in his defense. "Just a little unrestrained in anger management."
    The blonde muscle man who was his 'victim' is a locally-known blowhard from California. Everything is better in Pismo Beach, according to him, so everyone here on the Big Island wondered why he didn't just go back home. Apparently he has now done just that. Surfer Dude made bail and skipped town, but Kaleo will serve his time. For the next thirty days,

```
prison tats received in the Hamakua jail will
no doubt be of a distinctly higher grade.
```

Nani Palea was philosophical about the temporary closure of her brother's tattoo shop. She figured business would have been bad anyway. Even though the town did think he'd done the right thing, who'd trust her brother with their skin now?

Kaleo had told her – and the rest of Keawalani – all about it. Surfer Dude had swaggered into his shop, interrupting him in the midst of sketching a delicate hibiscus. The Californian had demanded a tattoo on the small of his back.

"What you want in such a hurry, *haole*?" Kaleo had asked using the not-necessarily-flattering term for a Caucasian mainlander.

Surfer Dude explained he wanted a naked chick who would bump and grind when he flexed his butt muscles. Wouldn't that be 'fuckin' awesome' undulating above his Speedo? He pointed out a girlie pattern he liked from the designs tacked to the Tat Joint's wall. For the next three hours, Kaleo worked. When at last he finished, he said, "Some of my best work, *haole*."

"I gotta see it."

"Not yet. Leave this bandage on it 'til you get to the beach then remove it and lie in the sun. Bright rays bring out the colors. Them beach babes gonna love it."

Kaleo was right. The women did love it when Surfer Dude unveiled his body art. They pointed and laughed. They made fun of his ass. That's how Surfer Dude discovered his tattoo was actually Kamapua'a, the Hawaiian Pig God, a porker best known for vulgar conduct.

When Surfer Dude busted in to confront the tattooist, a waiting customer called 911 before Kaleo could beat the snot out of the idiot. Police arrived and arrested them both.

Today, thirty days later, Kaleo was getting out so Nani was anxious to get to the Hamakua District jail. If she were late he'd start thumbing, and he'd be cranky enough as it was. But she couldn't rush Bethie Kalapana's feet. Bethie's tongue relaxed right along with her arthritic toes as Nani worked to loosen them. The brittle-boned woman was on the massage table, fussing about the new people who'd purchased the house just downhill from her own.

"She move da bonsai wikiwiki. Even before Martina Martin stay gone." Bethie used the pidgin English that was Hawaii's unofficial language, a rich stew from the immigrant populations who had settled the islands. Nani translated in silence. *She moved her bonsai plants in fast, even before Martina Martin moved out.*

Bethie's eyes were shut tight as Nani's talented hands manipulated hot stones to release the hammer toe. "Thirty da kine bonsai all over da lanai. Jacaranda ... shower tree ... all kine." The buyer of the Martin home came each day to water, prune and talk with her plants.

Nani understood that new neighbors were big news and no small cause for alarm, but she hurried the session as much as she could while still giving her client more than her money's worth. She believed in the art of touch, that all humans benefit from contact with others. Through massage or reflexology, she helped those around her with their physical woes.

What had surprised her early in her career was the amount of emotional woes that also came her way. Clients told her the most remarkable tales. Through no intent of her own, Nani Palea had become the Big Island secret keeper. Secrets that she kept, and sometimes even acted on, if she felt her involvement was justified.

Bethie finally climbed down from the table, slid into her *slippahs*, and wrote her check to Keawalani Hands.

"You know you need better support for your feet, Auntie," Nani said, using the respectful title for older women whether they were relatives or not. She said it well aware that flip flops were the only footwear Bethie would ever consider.

"*You* da support fo dese feet," the old woman said, stretching up to kiss Nani's cheek. Bethie was actually up on her toes. She could barely hobble before her session.

At last, Nani closed down her massage salon which was once the front bedroom of her house. She hurried out back and started up her Vespa. A car would have been better today, but the scooter was her only vehicle. It could just barely carry two when one was the size of her brother, Kaleo. He had customized her bike with a surrey top made from woven palm, and as long as she kept under 40 mph, the top stayed in place protecting her from sun or rain.

Excerpt from A TIME OF SECRETS

Nani putted through the village at slow speed then accelerated out the other side. Keawalani was far enough off the Big Island's beaten path that the air was still perfumed by plumeria more than by exhaust. Few tourists made it up the secondary road from Highway 19 to the village perched on the shoulder of Mauna Kea, the highest peak in the Pacific. If they did, they might stop for a pineapple shave ice at Halemano's Heavenly Treats or even a loco moco at the Big Island Girl, a diner whose signmaker had misheard the word *grill*. The islander attitude was "no worries" so Girl it remained.

After filling their bellies and maybe their fuel tanks, tourists moved on. There was no Hilo Hattie or Walmart to keep them or their money in the village. They traveled back down the road through cattle pastures to the highway and turned left toward Kona or right toward Hilo. It was the road that Nani took now, turning to the right to pick up her little brother, the convict. Kaleo had been in the slammer for thirty days sitting out his sentence. He'd been released to the custody of his big sister who was widely known to be the more dependable of the two.

Nani saw him walking along the side of the road and knew she was late. His boardshorts and tee-shirt looked a smidge tight. Prison food must have appealed to him. She'd get him off the fried rice and back on fresh fruit and mahi mahi.

"Aloha, bruddah," she said after she u-turned and pulled up next to him. They exchanged the Hawaiian embrace, kissing cheek to cheek. Then she placed a lei around his neck. "Welcome home." She'd made it from brown kukui nuts because they symbolized knowledge. Maybe some would actually rub off on her little brother.

"You're late," Kaleo griped. "I was released hours ago."

Okay, maybe knowledge will never rub off on him.

"You're welcome for picking you up at all."

Kaleo climbed aboard the Vespa behind her, grabbed hold of her waist and said, "You can drop me at the Tat Joint. I guess I'll stay there until I find someone to rent it. Hit it, *sistah*."

"No you don't, *bruddah*. According to the judge, you're coming home with me."

CHAPTER TWO

The Great Loco Moco Debate

By Jackson O'Reilly

Excerpt from the *Keawalani Voice,* 2012

This reporter was hanging with the boys down at Sunny Daze barber shop, awaiting a bi-monthly scalping. The conversation turned to loco mocos. Rumor has it this Big Island comfort food was invented in Hilo after WWII to keep the cholesterol of hungry guys climbing sky high.

"You gots to start with da good ground beef," Sunny claimed. "Not dat low fat crap." There was general agreement except from Motorhead who claimed to prefer his loco moco with pork or fish.

"But that ain't right," Sunny snapped back, snipping the air with his scissors. *(Note to readers: you don't want to make Sunny mad just before you get your haircut.)* "A real loco moco got da big scoop white rice under da burger patty, eggs sunny side and plenty brown gravy. No onions, mushrooms, kim chee, dat kine stuffs."

Excerpt from A TIME OF SECRETS

Vincent Moy revealed that his family's secret for a superior loco moco was bacon fat in the gravy, but others shouted him down using an unprintable phrase implying he didn't know poop from polish.

The battle raged over long or medium grain rice ... Worcestershire in the gravy or chili pepper water ... shoyu, Maui onion or daikon pickles as a condiment. But everyone did agree on two things:

First, the proper way to eat a loco moco is to break the eggs and blend with a bit of the meat, rice and gravy on your fork, then devour together in one ono bite after another.

Second, the best loco moco on the island can be had at the Big Island Girl. Asked later for a comment, Daya the Waitress said their secret ingredient was safe with her. She followed up with her enigmatic smile before gliding away to serve another round of the village's best coffee to her happy customers.

"Got any ice cream?" her little brother asked. 'Little' was misleading for Kaleo. True, he was twenty-six which made him three years younger than Nani. But at six foot four, he was ten inches taller. While he had the size of his Hawaiian ancestors, she'd inherited the slighter height of their Filipina great grandmother or maybe the Chinese plantation worker even farther back on their family tree. The Palea family, like most Hawaiians, was a mixed bag of backgrounds. *Chop suey* as the local slang went or *poi dogs* which meant mongrels.

Nani was a little brown dove of a woman who could best be called curvaceous. Her body wanted to be as lush as the island greenery, and it required as much maintenance to keep it trim. She wasn't crippled by body shame issues like so many of her *haole* sisters on the mainland, but she felt better when fit. It was easier to perform her job when her hands and arms were in peak condition.

Her round face was the perfect frame for an easily evoked smile. Her almond shaped brown eyes were as dark and welcoming as Kona coffee, yet an empathic spirit might divine the sadness always there, just behind the smile.

At long last, Nani's shiny black hair had outgrown the oddball slant created by Sunny Daze, the Keawalani barber. He disliked it when someone called him a stylist. Nani wouldn't make that mistake again. Snipping at the ends a bit at a time, she'd finally been able to even out the cut until her hair once again draped straight down to the middle of her back.

"There's frozen yogurt, non-fat vanilla," she said to her brother.

"Wailelenani. That is unfit food for a big man." Kaleo used her full name when she annoyed him. It meant *beautiful waterfall*. Her nickname, Nani, was common in the islands and simply meant *beautiful*.

"That man better not get any bigger if he doesn't want to look like a certain Pig Man himself." She believed he'd been making a few too many loco moco runs to the Big Island Girl.

By now Kaleo had been living in Nani's house for a couple weeks. He'd claimed the lanai so he would have his own back entrance without bothering Nani's clients who came through the front door. He'd busily framed in and screened its open walls, moved his bed into one end and reassembled his sound equipment along the other. Soon the entire residence – including Nani's massage table – vibrated with its volume. Their first argument had been over the use of headphones whenever clients were in the house.

Kaleo took on the job of doing all her spa sheets and towels since the washer and dryer were also on the lanai. The old machines seemed to dance along with him as music pounded through buds directly into his eardrums. He kept fresh Kona coffee brewing all day for her clientele, made sure there were plenty of water bottles in the fridge, chatted with clients who had to wait while Nani finished up a session, and took to answering Nani's phone to schedule appointments. He also launched into household maintenance, fixing the wobbly handrail out front, replacing a faucet washer and cutting the tough centipede grass with her hand mower.

Nani knew he was trying to earn his keep, and she appreciated most of his help. But she just never knew what change in routine awaited her each time she finished with a client. She was not pleased when he rearranged her kitchen cabinets to suit himself and updated her bookkeeping program. Now she could no longer find a frying pan or call up a balance sheet for Keawalani Hands Massage and Reflexology.

Today, Bethie Kalapana was back for her second appointment of the month. She was filled with news about the new neighbors soon to move in next door. "Martina Martin yard sale tomorrow den she goin' afta. Da peoples moving in wid all the bonsai name stay Yohay. I finally seen him first time oddah night. Now I get big problem, I tell you."

Bethie had begun to gesticulate with both hands while Nani decoded the pidgin: *Martina Martin was leaving right after she held a yard sale. The Yohays, who owned the bonsai plants, would then be moving in. Bethie had finally seen Mr. Yohay the other night, and now she had a problem.*

"You must keep still, Auntie Bethie," said Nani. She was trying to loosen the joints in the old woman's arthritic fingers. "Your hands are fluttering like 'i'iwi birds."

Bethie stopped her waving but continued her story. She had recognized Mr. Yohay as the boyfriend of her best friend, Likolani, who'd shown her a lovey-dovey photo of them together at the beach. "How you figgah? How he be husband of dis Miz Yohay *and* boyfriend of Likolani? I tink somethin' not right, yeah?"

"Hmmm. Sounds like one too many women to me," said Nani.

"How I tell my friend Liko? *Do* I tell her? She hate me for telling? For not telling? Auweeee." Bethie had worked herself into a snit again.

Nani knew her massage efforts would go to waste if the old woman didn't settle down. She thought about the problem for a moment then said, "I'll tell you what we will do, Auntie."

✦ ✦ ✦

After Bethie departed, Nani had a half hour before her next client. She padded barefoot to her kitchen for a cup of coffee. She was humming as she bent down in front of the fridge to get the low fat milk from the bottom shelf. While she was down there, she opened the crisper and rummaged around for one of the carrots she had cleaned. They had to be there. Kaleo wouldn't have touched them.

Now let's see ...

"Nani? We have a guest." Kaleo's voice was right behind her.

She shot straight up, slammed the refrigerator door on the gaping crisper drawer, opened it enough to shove the drawer back in, then whirled around as she kicked the door shut. Kaleo was sitting at the table in the breakfast nook with a smirk on his face and a stranger in a deep blue uniform sitting across from him. A stranger who'd just received a view of her blue jeaned butt gyrating to the Lady Gaga tune she was humming.

"Oh!" she said. "I didn't see you!" She glared at her brother who should have warned her.

The officer had a wide smile on his face as if he'd seen plenty of her. He stood and offered his hand. "I'm Officer Lindsey. You can call me Hank."

The handshake was a good one. Not the bone crusher she'd found common among men with a little authority. But not limp either. Firm and warm. She felt like the tropical temperature was rising. His face was all chiseled planes and sun browned skin and his pumped-up arms were ...

Maybe I better open the fridge again for a shot of cold air.

"It's the long arm of the law checking up on me," Kaleo said. "Hank here is the one who arrested me."

Nani bristled, tender thoughts of the cop dispersing. Any cop might bring back memories of that bad time years ago, of course. And this one had recently busted Kaleo. Her brother might be a pest, but he was family which made him *her* pest. "I assure you my brother is here all day long with me, helping run my business. He will be no further trouble to the law, Officer Lindsey."

"Glad to hear it, Ms. Palea. So you do massages here?"

Excerpt from A TIME OF SECRETS

Not the kind you're picturing, Officer Friendly. In a haughty tone she replied, "I am certified in Swedish, cranio-sacral and sports massage. As well as Thai, Danish and American reflexology."

The doorbell rang.

"Excuse me, officer, my next client is here. If you are through with my brother, he has work to do. I'll show you out." She turned to go then whipped back around. She wasn't giving him another rear view. "Please, after you."

Hank Lindsey must have substantial *haole* blood for his eyes to be that pure blue. They sparkled at her as if he saw right through the 'stick up her butt' routine.

Of course he would. He's a cop. He pries truth out of suspects.

His only parting shot was a smile that added laugh lines to those ocean blues. He went out the screen door as the village librarian scuttled in for her session. As Nani watched him go, she thought this cop was the most intriguing Big Island scenery she'd seen since cancelling her wedding two years ago.

Fo' shua!

END OF EXCERPT

Visit with Linda B. Myers at

www.LindaBMyers.com
facebook.com/lindabmyers.author
myerslindab@gmail.com
amazon.com/author/lindabmyers

Made in the USA
San Bernardino, CA
06 September 2017